YOUR ROOTS ARE SHOWING

A Novel

By Beverly Hayes Coleman

Arranged and published by the author Beverly Hayes Coleman

©2007 ISBN 978-0-6151-8249-0 Copyright by Beverly Coleman

www.lulu.com/yourrootsareshowing

©2007 ISBN 978-0-6151-8249-0

Acknowledgements

This book is dedicated to the people that have brought me the most joy that any one woman can have. Chenay, Kalli and Haili. Thank you so much for bringing joy and laughs to my heart and into my world. Everything I've ever done, I've done for you. God was preparing you for me, before you were even born, and we know that He always gets it right. To my family for your love and support that you've shown me over the years, thank you. To my Grandma for always expecting the best from me and making me feel like you're proud of me. It's an encouragement to keep going. To my closest sisters, Monay and Michelle, keep it cacklin'! I love yall! To my extended Christian family, the Mccarthy's, The Lowery's who adopted me, all everyone from the youngest to the oldest, thank you for continually praying for me all these years. Thank you, Auntie Marie, Uncle Kenny, Uncle George, Adroy, LV (may he rest peacefully), Darryl, and all the rest of my cousins. I want my brothers and sister to know that I love them very much, and the girls and I pray for you every night. To my mentor, Mr. Bernard Gipson, thank you for never having a rotten thing to say about me. (to my face) j/k. Thank you for supporting me and being the first to believe in me through thick and thin, sick and sin. God bless you! Thank you Don Mcclure with Creativfire for taking wonderful photos of me! And thank you to those employees of At&t who have encouraged me and spoke positively about my endeavors from beginning to end. Now mom, you know I can't forget about you. (cause I know you're saying, excuse me, what about me?) I saved the best for last. Thank you for bringing me into this world. I don't know everything you went through in your life, but I know that our steps are always ordered in the Lord. Thank you for doing whatever you thought was best for me, because you know what? It was. And finally, to my loving, fine, sweet, red bone husband. Thank you! Thank you! Thank you! You're not marrying me once, but you're marrying me twice! That says a lot about you brotha! I love you dearly and I always will. Thank you for my family, and thank you for encouraging me to "gwon-on" with my dreams! I love you.

Miami, FL

I hear and I function but I don't feel anymore. I don't feel a thing. What is this world coming to Lord? But most of all, what have I done? Trace looked around her and wondered what had brought her here. How had she gotten to this point in her life? Sure she had everything she wanted. But why couldn't she stop doing the things she did? Trace lay there staring out the window of her lavish but cozy apartment watching her next john come up the walkway. Trace seemed to have sold her soul to the devil and had no idea of how to get it back. She thought of ways to turn her life around but no time seemed like the right time. So, it never happened.

There came the knock at the door. The knock she expected. It used to be that that knock could mean love was possibly behind the door. She had given herself so freely that one day she thought she might fall in love with one of these men. But that never happened. Now it simply meant that there was some man wanting to sleep with her, no strings attached. Wanting her to make them feel like the world. In exchange there was no love, only pretense along with meaningless chatter that seems less and less interesting as the days wear on. Dirty money she didn't possibly need. Dirty money she didn't want and dirty men wanting to touch her. Years ago she would have frowned on a thing like this but now there was nothing left. There was nothing with which she could hold on to. Only her daughter. Her sweet daughter, who wasn't a baby anymore and didn't need her mom all the time. That didn't matter now. What mattered was the fool knocking softly on the door again waiting to see the other side. "Come in" she yelled, as sweetly as she could. "Don't beat the damned door off baby." When the door opened, Trace couldn't believe her eyes. Her next john was the man who should have been her husband many years ago. "Oh Lord. What have we here!?" he exclaimed.

She walked over to the stereo and turned it down a bit. She didn't feel like hearing these melancholy love songs right now. "Close your mouth Jeronn and tell me why you're here. What can I do for you?" He didn't reply. He couldn't.

"Well don't just stand there. What do you want?" She was trying to remain calm. He just stood there and stared in shock at the woman he used to love so much. Hell, whom was he fooling? He still loved her. Lately he couldn't seem to get her off his mind. But what was she doing here and what had she become? They stared into each other's eyes, knowing the answer to his question. He knew why she was here. It was all over her face. The only words he could utter were.. "Baby let me take you home." He spoke quietly and gently. He wanted to make her feel that she had done nothing terribly wrong so she would not feel ashamed about him finding her there. As Trace stood there looking into the reality of his eyes, she suddenly knew where this all began. How she came to be a lonely part time prostitute. Tears swelled in the rims of her eyes and not falling before she turned away from him in shame. He knew it and she knew it all at once. Trace had gone too far and too fast!

Chicago, Illinois

Chapter One

"Mama guess what? I made the cheerleading team!" Trace was so happy she could pop. "That's good baby, now move you standing in front of the TV." "Ok mama. What you cookin' for dinner?"

"I'm making some chili. Go do your homework or something." Trace's mom did not like to be bothered when she's watching General Hospital. "I don't have any homework mama it's Friday and I'm practically in 9th grade."

"Well get outta my way I'm watching my stories now." Trace went and sat on the porch. She heard her mother shout behind her.. "and don't be out there talking to that bad ass boy neither, or I'll make you come in the house." Trace just rolled her eyes. She hadn't even seen Joseph in two days. She could still hear her mother talking to no one at all. "I hope he in jail, the lil' red bastard. That's where he belong!" She makes me sick, Trace thought to herself. Damn she gets on my nerves. She always hollerin' about something too. She holler too damned much. "What's wrong with you?" Just then her friend Aaron sat on the porch.

"Oh hi Ay. Nothing's wrong with me. My mother is always complaining.

You know how she is. She always got to say something about something and she starting to get on my nerves. I mean all she does is sit on her butt watching t.v. all day and barking orders at everybody."

"Oh well you might as well forget about that. That's what parents are put on this earth for." "What are you doing here? Why aren't you at football practice or something?"

"I didn't feel like going. It's too hot." They sat there looking around at all the houses, the sun, and the sky. Trace lived on the south side of Chicago. A pretty decent neighborhood compared to some she's seen. Not too much violence around here. But you could find a crack dealer on every other corner. There was the occasional stupid fight here and there but for the most part a nice neighborhood. Trace's block was the only block in the neighborhood that had all houses. There were no buildings or flats. Most people on her block cared for their lawns and their houses. They took pretty good care of the neighborhood too. They always had fun block parties, which she hadn't paid much attention to now that she was getting older.

"Schools out next week," she said. "Then you'll have plenty of time for the sun." She couldn't think of much else to say to Aaron. He was a cute guy. He was one of the cutest in the whole neighborhood. And he liked her too. But her heart was somewhere else.

"Anyway," he finally spoke. "Where's your boyfriend at?"

"Joseph ain't my boyfriend and I don't know where he's at." "Then how you know that's who I'm talking about?"

"Because everybody says he's my boyfriend."

"I heard he's got another girlfriend and she's even older than you and him." Traces' heart sank. She felt like a barefaced idiot in front of Aaron because she had heard the same thing too. "I don't care. He ain't my boyfriend anyway." After defending herself, she decided to save face by changing the subject. "Guess what? I made the cheerleading team."

"So, schools out next week and you graduating so what big accomplishment is that?"

"Not for eighth grade dummy for high school. They have freshman try-outs at the end of school year for the following year and I went there and made the team." She sighed. He bored her. "And now I'm going in the house now because I have some make up homework to do if I want to graduate." She lied. Trace wanted to be alone. Her good news seemed short-lived since everybody in the whole world knew that Joseph had another girlfriend. 'Why am I always getting my feelings hurt?' she thought.

"Alright, I'm going over my homey crib anyway and I'll call you later tonight alright?" 'Whatever' thought Trace. Aaron was cute, but she couldn't relate to him. There wasn't enough to him. For some reason, she always ended up liking the boys who didn't care much about nothing. She wasn't a bad looking girl herself. Maybe a little shy and reserved, but for the most part she felt she was pretty all right. She always thought her complexion to be a little too dark but she thought of herself as pretty okay for the most part.

Trace went into her room. She felt like screaming. Not too loud though so her wicked witch mother wouldn't hear her. She felt so stupid and used. Part of her knew she shouldn't care about Joseph and his new girlfriend. Her mother said Joseph was too old for her anyway. She was thirteen and wouldn't be fourteen until summer was over. Joseph was 16 and would be 17 at the end of the summer. According to her mother he'd always be too old for her. Joseph always seemed to make her cry too for one reason or another. He was rude and disrespectful to a lot of people. Most of the kids in the neighborhood hated him because he acted like a bully. Most boys were afraid to fight him. He just had a bad rep no matter how you looked at it. But she wanted him for some reason. He made her feel good. Inside and outside. He made her laugh a lot and that's always what she looked forward to. Him making her laugh. That's what she thought she needed. She would always feel miserable when they would break up. At thirteen, she felt more like a woman than anybody knew. She was having all the desires of a woman, or so she thought. So it was no small thing when they would break up. In her mind, her world was over. She would never be able to talk to her mother about such things. Her mother frightened her. In some ways, she felt her mother didn't care what she did, but on the other hand she felt her mother watched everything she did. "Trace, come down here and eat!" her mother shouted up the stairs. "I'm not hungry!" she yelled back. "Get your ass down here and eat because I'm not gone heat it up again!" "Ugh!" she gritted her teeth "I hate her and she's always yelling." She said to no one. She threw her stuffed animal aside and went to the bathroom to wash her face. She couldn't wait to see Joseph. Where was he anyway when she needed him? They would sit on the porch and talk and talk when her mother wasn't home. And she knew he would be the one person who would care that she made the cheerleading team for high school. Trace walked downstairs where her cousins were already sitting down eating. Her aunt was in her room sleeping her life away as usual. She never came out except to go in the bathroom and go to work.

She sat down and ate in a hurry. She wanted to get outside. She hated living in this house. She always felt that everyone else had the better house, better parents, better everything. She used to wish she were adopted. Sometimes life at home wasn't that bad. Sometimes it was actually happy. But with a teenager in love and going through changes, those things didn't matter. She went outside to see if Joseph were anywhere around. She didn't want to miss him just in case he came past her house. I can't wait to grow up and become rich and famous, she thought to herself. All she could think of right now is.. 'I hate this house.'

The whole weekend went by and Trace waited and waited but there was no sign of Joseph. She was becoming furious and trying to make herself hate him. As she was getting ready for school she looked at herself in the mirror. She hated her hair. It's so puffy looking she thought. Her mother said she could have a perm when she reached 13, but that hadn't happened yet. Of course her mother wasn't paying for her to get perm. Promises, promises. She did the best she could with it in a pony tail and bangs, deeply wishing it to grow longer and straighter and to be as pretty as some of the other girls in school. "When I become a movie star," she said to the mirror while holding the sides of her face, "I'm gone have long and beautiful hair and it'll never look like this again." "Hurry up and get outta here." came the familiar order from her mother. "Go on 'fore you be late." Trace left. When she got to the corner she smiled. This would be the last day at school for eighth graders and she would never walk this way to school again.

By the end of the day in class some of the kids were crying because this would be the last time that they all saw each other and most of the class had been together since the third grade. Including Trace. Graduation was Friday and some of the kids weren't even coming. Some were moving away already and some were leaving to visit relatives in other states for the summer. Trace was a little sad too. It wasn't because she wouldn't see these kids again. It was because she wasn't doing anything special for graduation. She was showing up on Friday with what few students who would be there and after that it's back home. Soon everyone was passing around signature books. To say goodbye in words to the people they had grown up with. It seemed to her that not many books were passed her way. She didn't care. She just wanted to go home and start summer. It was almost twelve o'clock and time to go. Trace was still glancing through her signature book when she got to one of the last pages. She stared at it. She read it over and over. She couldn't believe that someone could be so mean. They didn't sign their name, but she felt like all eyes were on her. She stood up and ran out of the class with tears in her eyes. She wasn't going to let them see her cry. She ran into the hall hearing her teacher call after her. She started running down the stairs wondering if she should go back. She looked at the book again. She couldn't. She turned around with one last goodbye to the school and halls she had known for the past six years. She didn't care anymore. She ran all the way home wondering how could her last day of school be the worst.

She ran to her room and slammed the door, which wasn't that easy considering the thick, ugly green carpet on the floor. She flopped on her bed and read the words again. "Trace, I have known you since third grade and you're still a quiet and cool person. The only thing you should change is your clothes. Don't dress like a bum in high school or they'll laugh you out." Even saying it out loud she couldn't believe it. She tried to figure out who wrote it. She really didn't recognize the writing. Obviously it was disguised. Trace went downstairs to show her mother in the hopes that maybe she'll feel sympathetic enough to make her feel better by buying her some new clothes. She hoped. She shook her mother who was on the couch nodding off about to miss her soaps. Cautiously she woke her afraid she might get yelled at for doing so.

"Mama, wake up, I got something to show you. Look what somebody wrote in my book." Her mother rolled over on the couch drowsily and squinted at the words through her sleepy eyes, yawning like she really didn't have time for this. Her mother looked up at her with blaming eyes. "You woke me up for this!?" she spoke unconcerned. "Girl, if you don't get out my face with this bullshit." And she just turned over and went back to sleep. Just like that. Trace couldn't believe her mother. She turned up her lip in disbelief.

"I don't believe it." she spoke out. "You're mad at me?? Somebody wrote these mean words to me and you're mad at me??" She stomped to the door. "I hate her," she growled.

She sat on the porch, which she was beginning to hate more and more now that she was really mad at her mother. She heard someone calling her name and she had to shield her eyes from the sun to see who was standing across the street. It was Joseph and he was coming over to her. Joseph was always somewhere doing something. He dropped out of school recently but he didn't think she knew. Her heart was racing as he came towards her. All she knew is that Joseph would make her feel better. He would take all her anger away and make her laugh and smile and be happy. As he came closer though something caught her attention that made her heart hurt so bad she thought it would explode. Joseph had a hickey on his neck the size of a quarter and as red as strawberry Kool-Aid. She couldn't take this. She got up and walked in the house as if he wasn't even there.

Chapter Two

"Trace wake up, wake up. Joseph is downstairs on the porch for you."

"What time is it?" "It's nine-thirty." It was her cousin Natrice.

"You been sleep all day."

"What does he want? Don't he know what time it is?"

"I don't know but you better come down before your mama come." Trace

woke right up then. Her mother. She was still mad at her. She was a little

nervous about going downstairs though. She turned on the light and

looked in the mirror. She pushed her hair back and went downstairs

quietly so her mom wouldn't hear. She jumped the last step cause she

knew it would creak if she stepped on it. Her cousin was the only person

she could talk to sometimes. Even though they lived downstairs. They

were still cool though. When she reached the bottom she could see

Joseph standing on the inside porch smiling.

"What do you want?" She stared at his pale yellow skin and big black

eyes. He had gold hair. She felt this was a special thing to be such a light

skinned black man with gold curly hair especially since she was dark

skinned. She knew, even at her young age that she had a complex about it

but it didn't matter to her. What mattered was the fact that Joseph had

risked her mother cursing him out to see her. What mattered was he had come looking for her and even though she wouldn't tell him, she was happy about it. When he smiled he had the prettiest teeth. He was like sunshine to her. He had the fullest pinkest lips she'd ever seen on someone black. Or maybe she never noticed it before. He was almost three years older than her but that didn't matter, she was in love. He was her first at everything. She loved him like she knew she would never love anyone else. To Trace, Joseph was the world.

"What do you want?" Trace asked. She tried to seem unconcerned. Like having Joseph there really wasn't what she wanted. He pulled her close to him. *That's better* she thought. With Joseph, age didn't matter. She knew she was too young to be doing what she did with him, but she couldn't help it. It felt good. Around Joseph she felt nervous but she felt good. She loved it. She wanted to feel this way. She really adored him. Whenever Joseph was around she could be the girl she thought she was in her mind. She stepped out onto the inside front porch and closed the front door.

"Be quiet," she warned, "or my mother will hear you."

"Man Trace," he sighed. "You lookin' good in them shorts." He was checking her out. She liked it. "Listen Trace, I don't wanna wait anymore. Just lemme pull your shorts down baby. I promise, it's gone

feel good." Before she could object, he kept talking and caressing.

"Just take one leg out. Come on." "Look, Joseph, I know how it's done

and I don't wanna do it. So don't try and make me okay?"

"Gimme a kiss," she kissed him quickly. It was nice. But she wanted to

do whatever she could to slow him down anyway. And she really didn't

want him waking up her mother. Both their lives would be over. She also

didn't want him to leave to go and be with some other girl. He became

more aggressive and she started to get nervous. "Come on Joseph. Just

stop before my mother comes downstairs." *That's it. Put the fear of God*

in him by bringing up my mother. She tried to ease the situation by

changing the subject but that didn't stop him. "What about your other

girlfriend Joseph?" But Joseph wasn't listening to her. He started rubbing

her breasts, small though they were, and hardly a caress. It felt good but it

also hurt and scared her at the same time. *This fool is not listening to me,*

she thought. She asked again. "What about her Joseph?" It was more of a

command this time. He was kissing her neck and rubbing her all over. It

felt good. Too good for a young girl. She let him do it. It was as if the

further she let him go, the more he answered her questions and she wanted

the answers. She needed to know what was going to happen between

them. When he finally pulled his pants down he only whispered, "Denise and I broke up." She wanted to believe him with all her heart but then there was that ickey hickey right there on his neck. He was lying and Trace hated to be lied to. It tore her inside when someone lied to her. She tried to make him feel guilty about the hickey by asking him if he wanted her to suck on the same spot, but he just ignored her. He wasn't even listening to her. It was as if she weren't even there. They were having sex, right there in the hallway, standing up and somehow she knew this was it. She knew that he didn't break up with Denise and there was nothing she could do to make him want to stay with her. Not even giving herself to him would work. She felt so stupid with him not saying a word and that made her feel more mad and hurt at the same time.

When it was over, she fixed her clothes and waited. She stared at him. She wanted him to say something. She wanted him to feel guilty about using her that way. She asked him if it meant they were back together and he just looked at her. He opened the door without answering. "Joseph?" She felt the tears swell up as she internally panicked. Was she going have to be a drama queen and beg him to stay? She could feel the pain in the back of her throat as she tried not to cry, though she knew she would. But she didn't want him to see her cry. "I'm sorry." was what he said. "I shouldn't have done that." '*Excuse me?*' She thought. "What?" she protested. But she knew what was coming next. He was going to walk out the door and leave her as quickly as he came feeling stupid and used. "Joseph, please don't do this to me." *That was almost begging*, she thought. He walked down the steps turned around and looked her in the eyes and spoke words that she would probably never forget for as long as she lived, "Thanks for the pussy." He was laughing. He walked away as if she just loaned him a dollar.

"What?" she hissed. She didn't want to shout so she wouldn't wake up her mother.

"What are you talking about?" She was getting angry. He kept walking as if she wasn't there. She wanted to run after him and curse him out but she was too afraid of her mother hearing her. Or a neighbor telling her mother what they saw so she ran upstairs to her room. She cried herself to sleep and wished so hard that she could talk to her mother or someone about this. Even if she could, what would she say? That night she made a vow to herself to never be that gullible again. To Joseph or any body else. That night Trace truly became a woman.

Chapter Three

Four years later

"Bye mama, I'm going to church." Trace opened her mom's door but she wasn't there. Actually she hadn't been there all night. Trace's mother seemed to change and Trace didn't know why. Her mother's baby who had come along a year ago was downstairs with her cousins so he was fine. Trace went downstairs to the kitchen and still didn't see her mother. "Natrice, you seen my mama?" Natrice rolled her eyes. "Nope and I'm tired of watching your baby brother." Trace frowned.

"Trace, don't act like you don't know what's going on here." Trace didn't know.

"What's going on?" she asked.

"Nothing just forget it." "No I wanna know. Tell me what's going on?" "Trace why do you think Big James left your mother huh?" Big James was her little brothers' father. He had been with her mother all during her high school years. They really seemed to be getting along fine, but then one day he just packed all his stuff and left. One day Trace came home from her after school job and he was gone. Trace really didn't know what happened because she didn't speak to her mother much at all these past few years. "Trace you been walking around here being all saved and sanctified and sticking your head in the Bible every five minutes, you haven't paid attention to what's happening right under your nose. Look at your mother. Look how skinny she done got. Can't you see she's on drugs? I notice it. My sister notices it. My mother notices it. It's *your* mother! How come you don't notice it? You go on to church today and tell God to open your eyes girlfriend. Ya mama smoking crack and she's killing herself right before your eyes. And don't tell me you didn't know she was pregnant again?"

Trace was in shock. She didn't realize any of these things about her mother. She couldn't even think back to decide when it had all come about. This isn't something that happened to a strong, mean woman such as her mother. She didn't know what to say while Natrice stood there rolling her eyes and twirling her neck as she spoke.

"What?" she finally squeaked.

"Yeah Trace, your mother's pregnant. Uh-gen!"

"You watch your damn mouth and don't ever say anything like that again about my mother!!" she yelled.

"Oh what? You curse now?? The Holy Ghost just left ya just like that huh? You open your eyes girl. I love your mother just like you do. She's as much a mama to me as she is to you since my mother can't do nothing but sleep all day. I hurt for her Trace but I can't hide it no more. That's all

I got to say." Trace was angry. She couldn't wait to see her mother. She was finally going to stand up to her. She was so mad she didn't feel very holy inside. She was hurt and angry. The strong woman that she could never talk to had turned into something she hadn't even known about. She went to church and prayed for forgiveness for all the things she was going to say to her mother. She told one of her friends at church what she had found out and they prayed for her too. Trace never felt real love until she joined the church. This was her home now. Where she belonged. She cried hard but it felt good. She went home and found Natrice and Nesha watching TV.

"Where's my mother?" "Upstairs." they answered in unison, not turning away from the big screen television. "And she got company." Natrice yelled back. She walked slowly up the stairs listening for anything. She didn't know what she was listening for but she was trying. When she turned to the landing the baby was at the top of the stairs holding a bottle and wearing a soaking diaper. She laughed to herself. That little boy was so cute. But she could see her mother must be turning straight ghetto. He giggled when he saw her. He grinned showing his four little teeth but not quite taking that bottle far away from his little mouth. His little t-shirt was soaking from baby slobber and milk but he was happy. She tickled his little fat feet and called out to her mother. She heard someone shuffling in her mother's room and waiting. Her mother opened the door. Trace looked shocked at the look on her mothers face. This didn't look like her mother at all. She was not plump and daring and mean looking. Her mother's lips were all white and her eyes were all bugged out her head like she had seen a ghost. She looked worried like she wasn't safe in her own bedroom. Trace was afraid of what she saw. And what was that smell coming from the room? It smelled as if no one in that room had washed for days. Trace wasn't hurt or angry. She felt disappointed. She felt let down. All the energy she had to speak up to her mother faded away. She felt let down and afraid at that moment and she wondered whether or not she really cared. She felt defeated. What could she do? She didn't know a thing about drugs or drug treatment, so what could she say? She just really didn't know.

"Mama," she spoke softly, "Jr. is wet."

"Well change him for me!" she almost begged.

"What are you doing?" Trace asked. "And what is that smell coming out of your room?" Trace was angry with her mother.

"Stop being so damned nosey and change him for me." She closed the door. Trace picked up the baby and walked down the hall to her own room. After she washed and changed the baby she gave him a warm bottle and put him to sleep. She sat on the floor by her door and listened quietly to what was going on in her mom's room. The door was cracked. She could still see what was going on inside. She noticed how skinny her mom was getting which made it easier to see the bulge in her stomach. The man in the room didn't notice Trace watching and neither did her mom. His mind was on the pipe in his hand. If they had noticed, they didn't seem to care. But how could she not notice? Trace thought. How could she not even feel me watching her? She didn't notice Trace when she lit the fire. She didn't notice Trace as she inhaled that awful smelling smoke. And she didn't notice Trace when Trace began to cry. She only noticed the pipe in her hand. Trace knew from then on she no longer had a reason to even try to look up to her mother. I'm gone be somebody one day she thought. I'm gone leave here and never come back. Trace decided to take another job that was offered to her at a restaurant by one of the ministers in her church. She would save more money and leave her mother forever.

Back in Miami

Present Day

"Trace baby let me take you home." He reached for her hand. She let him hold it for a moment before she pulled it away.

"Trace! Just tell me what's going on here? What are you doing here?" She couldn't speak. She was feeling so high from the joints she had smoked before he got here. She almost wanted to laugh at him standing there. "Trace, I don't understand. Help me to understand." He waited. "I mean you're a beautiful, wealthy woman. I just wanna know what you're doing here." He wasn't getting any answers from her. *I don't owe him a thing*, she thought. She just stood there looking so sexy to him in her long silk robe. It went so well with her beautiful brown skin. He wanted to hold her. He hadn't seen her in so long and she looked so damned good. "Where's Chanelle?" he asked. She crooked her head at the nerve of his question.

"Don't you ever ask about my daughter!" was all she said to him. After finally getting a good look at him Trace realized this man looked better today than he did 10 years ago. The brother was fine. Not a hair out of place. His skin was just as butter as she remembered. He wore a dark colored suit with a black shirt. His style was impeccable as usual. He could always outdress her. No matter how many clothes she bought he would win in the fashion department on the best dressed. The man was cool. She could also see in glancing that he wasn't wearing a wedding ring. That must be why he's here, she thought.

"She's in school Jeronn. Where the hell do you think she is?" She tried to sound indignant. But the excitement of Jeronn Clarke being right here in front of her after all this time did something to her knees. It also did something to her heart.

"What do you want here anyway?" She asked.

"Well I think I know what you want, but why are you here? You left me a long time ago and now you want to know how I'm doing? Well as you can see I'm doing just fine?" If she didn't stop talking now she knew she would start babbling. She was too high. "Trace, may I sit down?" The words oozed off his sweet tongue like honey. "I would like to talk to you for a minute if I may." He said this while easing down on her cream leather sofa. Trace sat down in the chair across from him. She didn't want to sit too close to him. Her heart couldn't take that. As Jeronn looked around the beautiful apartment, he realized there was no sign of poverty here. There was nothing to suggest that Trace needed to be here. He didn't quite understand why she was here. The paintings on the wall themselves were worth a pretty penny. The stereo system, even the neighborhood the apartment was in was upper crust. The apartment was immaculate. She didn't look like she needed to sleep with men for money. Jeronn was having a real hard time with this. Maybe he had the wrong apartment and came to her by chance. They began to stare at one another. She pulled her hosed feet under her long silk gown waiting for him to speak.

He still looked as sexy and gorgeous as he did the night they met. She eyed him from head to toe again. It was a shame that he still had this effect on her. It made her feel sexy just staring at him. He came over on his knee and took her hand and softly rubbed it. She let him. It had been a long time since anyone showed any real affection and coming from Jeronn it felt nice. "Trace" he spoke softly. "Baby, again, I don't understand. I would never have expected to find you in here." He didn't know where to begin. He knew she had a short temper so he spoke carefully. "Trace, whose place is this?"

"Mine," she turned her mouth up as if to say 'now what?' He looked around. The apartment definitely had her style. She always had good taste in decorating. "Trace, Honey, why are you here? You have no need to be here. You have everything you need. You have people who love you, people who care about you. Your fans adore you. Me, I adore you. What would people say if they knew you were here? What would they say if they found out Trace Reese was a whore?" *No he didn't!* She got off that chair so fast you could hear the wind. She slapped him. "You lousy bastard! You son of a bitch! You can get the fuck out of here the same way you came in. What gives you the right to judge me huh?" She was looking him square in the eyes. Not really raising her voice. She was a star. She didn't sweat. "What would your fucking wife say if she found out her perfect assed husband came to visit a whore huh?? You lousy son of a bitch! You get the hell out of here. You haven't changed. Still fucking around. The same way you left me. You're no better than me. I don't need you. Get out!" She finally screamed. She went to the bathroom and slammed the door. The radio was playing Mariah Carey's song "I Still Believe". Jeronn loved that song. He hadn't written any new songs in quite awhile. He was beginning to hate the radio. He poured himself a brandy while he waited for her to return from the bathroom. He knew he shouldn't have said what he said but he was at a lack for words and so shocked at Trace. He didn't know what else to do or say. He knew why he had really come here, but she didn't. He just hadn't expected to find her here. He swallowed his drink in one gulp before realizing she wasn't coming out as long as he was there. He was sorry he had bumped into her like that. He looked around the apartment drinking in her scent. He looked at the bathroom once more. He walked out without saying good-bye. Damned his heart hurt.

Jeronn went down to his car. He looked up at the window of her apartment. Maybe she would be looking at him. She was. They stared at each other for quite awhile. He wanted to run back up and beg her to forgive him. Beg her to forgive him for the past. For today. He was remembering all the things they had been through together. He felt like a fool finding her there after the way he left her for his now ex-wife. He had walked out on her. He had come to Florida with high hopes and big dreams and when those dreams started to come true, he left his woman for another. They stared at each other in silence and through the drizzle that was now coming down making it hard to see. She still loved him and she knew it. She would always love Jeronn. He was her man. They both stood there....remembering the night they met.

Chapter Four

Chicago, IL

Years ago

Trace walked into the club with her friend Mikah. She felt so nervous from wearing a short mini dress. It was a far cry from the long church dresses she wore just a couple of years ago. It was amateur night at Club 2000 and she was going to sing. Mikah had heard there would be a talent agent there that night and had dragged her friend there because she knew of her big dreams of becoming a star. She wanted Trace to make it. Trace deserved some happiness. They sat down at the bar, preferring it to a table. That way they could see everyone coming in. It made her feel good when men would double take a look at her. She knew she was fine in her black dress. Even though she had just had a baby a year earlier her body was the bomb. She didn't have any complaints. She felt a little nervous about singing though. It was almost 10:30 and it was time for the show to start. She and Mikah ordered drinks and watched from the bar. She didn't know what she had ordered. She just asked for whatever the person next to her had. It looked good so why not. Trace thought about her beautiful baby at home and told herself that she was doing this for her. She was going to become a star and give her baby everything in the world she needed. At one year old, her baby was already doing things that much older babies would be doing. Her baby girl was pretty and smart and all the things she'd hoped her baby would be. She always felt good when she thought about her baby girl. Her baby girl would be her good luck charm tonight, she thought. She couldn't believe her sorry baby's daddy claimed to love her and making promises of marriage could be such a conniving little liar. The drink was making her feel so good. Her nerves were much calmer now. There were quite a few people packed inside this club. She ordered a couple of Zinfandels for her and Mikah. She felt real good now. "Slow down girl, or you won't be able to stand up and sing," laughed Mikah. She laughed too. "Girl please, I'm fine." She noticed the bartender smiling at her so she smiled back. Here I go again she thought. Flirting with another loser, she laughed to herself. By now Mikah had had the attention of several guys at the bar and she was hardly dressed as scantily as Trace, she thought. Mikah was a pretty woman. She had long black hair, the kind that never needed a perm. It was in her blood. Everybody in her family had that kind of hair. She had a beautiful light skinned complexion. Never had any acne for as long as Trace knew her. She never needed to wear make up either. She was blessed with beautiful skin. She did wear hot red lipstick once in awhile, but for the most part, Mikah was gorgeous. She had some hips though. Men seemed to love those hips. The bartender came over and offered to buy her a drink, which she easily accepted.

"What's your name?" he asked. "Trace." she replied. "I guess your friends call you T right?" "No, but you can," she was flirting big time. *What's my problem*? She thought. He smiled. "My name is Nate. My mother owns this place."

"Oh really? That's nice." She couldn't think of a thing to say. "So I guess you buy drinks for every girl that comes in here and smiles at you huh?" she teased.

"No. Only the pretty ones," he teased.

"Well at least your honest. Is this your only job?"

"Why? You want my paycheck?" They both laughed.

"Very funny, I'm just asking."

"You're trying to figure out how much I make so you can get half right? I know about women like you." He laughed. "No you didn't!" She laughed. She looked at Mikah and was pretending to ignore him now. "Wait girl, I'm just kidding," he said

"I know. It's cool." Just then she heard them call her name to the stage. Mikah turned to her. "This is it girl."

"Mikah, I'm so nervous."

"Do your best girl." As she turned to leave Nate wished her luck as well.

She handed the DJ her tape and made her way to the stage. Her nerves were on edge, but she could handle it. She started to sing "Black Butterfly" by Denise Williams. By the time she got to the end of her song, she noticed a pair of eyes in the audience staring at her, surrounded by an angel- hunk wearing a white linen suit. She figured he must have been the talent agent coming to hear all the acts. With that in mind she ended the song in a way that made the crowd scream. Trace loved it. No one ever clapped this much for her. Not even in church. She walked from the stage gracefully. People were grabbing her arms and congratulating her. She looked around but the man was gone. *'Where is he'?* she thought. She made her way to Mikah. "Where is he?" she asked.

"You were great! Where's who?"

"The talent agent."

"Oh, he's over there in the black suit," she answered.

"That's not him." "Yes it is. Why do you think everybody's in his face?"

"Well where's the guy th...never mind. Anyway, so was I good girl?"

"I told you homey, you in the money!!" They laughed. "My girl gone be rich one of these days."

Instinctively, she felt someone right behind her. And just as quickly, she knew it was the fine looking brother she had seen when she was on stage. She could feel him behind her. She couldn't turn around. She looked straight ahead at nothing in particular with a smirk on her face. She couldn't turn around though. This vibe was too stimulating. Then it came. The softest, sweetest, deepest, sexiest voice she'd ever heard in the English language, was speaking to her. "Was that song for me?" it asked.

She felt just like Diana Ross when Billy Dee Williams asked her 'You gone let me arm fall off?' in Lady Sings the Blues. She held her breath. His breath smelled so sweet next to her face. She could only hear him even though the music was blasting. She barely turned around. She felt unworthy of looking at such a fine brother in the face. "Maybe," she spoke seductively. "What's your name?" he asked. He was too real to lie to so she gave him her real name. "Trace, and yours?"

"What would you like it to be?"

"I really don't care." She gave him the hand in the face, while turning her back to him completely once more. Trying to seem uninterested. She didn't know his eyes would be so sparkly and electrifying. "They were clearer than the drink she was drinking to calm her nerves. "Well then, I guess I have to tell you. Its Jeronn." he stumbled.

"You didn't sound like you were sure of that," she said.

"Well, it's a shorter version of my real name, but then I'd have to stand here for an hour and explain my real name to you and I don't feel like going that route right now. You sing very well." he changed the subject.

"Thank you," she answered.

"It's getting late. Shouldn't a little girl like you be getting home by now?" She turned around and faced him fully.

"Excuse me? How old do you think I am?" She put on her prettiest, but not too eager smile ever. "Don't matter really," he answered.

"But I know you're not old enough to be in here." She almost fell to the floor. She didn't know someone could be so big and beautiful up close. She wanted him bad. "I refuse to let you talk to me like a baby so don't even try that with me lover. But I do think you're right, I should be getting home. I've done what I came to do anyway." Oh she just knew she was a hot mama now. She turned away and began looking for Mikah around the room. "Hold on girl! You don't have to be like that. You got a man at home waiting for you or something?" She just looked at him and turned away. He licked his pretty lips and pulled himself to the seat in front of her and sat down. "I was making an offer but I guess it didn't quite come out right." She cocked her head to the side and gave him a look like she was trying to figure him out. "Why don't I take you home huh? How about that?" She turned her head and squinted while contemplating the thought. Not knowing whether she should trust this pretty boy or not. "Well my friend's here with me." she exhaled. "She lives down the street and I'm going to stay at her house tonight. "Well, why don't you let me

take your friend home and take you to get some breakfast or something."
That sounded so much better to her. After all, he was the finest man she'd
ever seen and it seems like everyone at this club seems to know him.
"Okay." she said. "But let me get my tape and my friend and I'll meet you
outside."

Having breakfast with Jeronn was a good idea. He was very smart and
had a lot of bright ideas. He was not just a pretty face. She liked him a
lot. She tried to keep her cool as much as she could. She entertained the
thought of sleeping with him but she didn't clue him in on her thoughts.
The time flew by and before you know it they were leaving IHOP and
heading back to her place. "Thank you for breakfast. It was nice and
thank you for bringing me home."
"Well it doesn't have to be over does it? I could walk you to your door
and make sure everything is okay inside."
"I'm sure it is, so that's okay." she replied, not really wanting him to give
up. Throughout the night and even at the restaurant she was trying to
avoid those eyes. They were so intense. You would think he had on
mascara his lashes were so thick. But at the restaurant she could see that
they were just plain old beautiful eyes. She knew that if she weren't
careful she would give her soul to this man. Even on their first night

together.

"You know, you're certainly a lot shier than I expected you to be."

"Well, what did you think I was? A floozy right? It's this dress?" she asked.

"No baby it's not the dress. That dress is all that and so is the woman in it?"

"Oh so I'm a woman now huh?" she teased. "I'm not a little girl anymore like you were treating me at the club?"

"That remains to be seen."

"Excuse me?" He leaned over and kissed her. It was good. It was soft and wet and nothing like she had expected. It was real. It was warm.

"Would you like to come in Jeronn?"

"I don't know. Where's the shy lady, I was just beginning to like?" he asked. She smiled. "You just kissed her good night." When she took her heels off she was a lot shorter and he looked a lot bigger. All over. He turned her around and unzipped her dress. They were wasting no time. She could see that the passion she had inside, he also possessed it and they couldn't wait to get to each other.

"This has to be the sexiest black dress I've ever seen on a woman," he spoke softly. There was that voice again in her ear. It made her back tingle. "Mmm," she moaned. She arched her back and gently pulled his hips to her. Not wanting to wait for the love that was about to be made. She couldn't remember ever feeling so good. "Oh Jeronn," she moaned. He was rubbing her everywhere. She felt so alive in his arms. When they were both completely naked they stared at each other. Since neither had bothered to find any light, all they had was the moon shining through the sheer curtains to guide them to each other. She stared at his sexy abs. He stared at her feminine curves. She looked so soft to him he could barely touch her. His skin glowed in the moonlight. And he could see every detail of her ebony body. She was so beautiful and sensuous that it was all he could do to keep from consuming her in one breath. He looked at her stomach. He looked in her eyes.

"You have children." He said more as a statement than a question. "Yes," she whispered. "How many?" His deep musky voice, barely a whisper. He wanted her feel that she needn't have any inhibitions during what they were about to do. He didn't realize when they were eating that this woman could interest him so much, but here they were and he couldn't wait to have her. "Does it matter how many at this moment?" She whispered. She was anticipating his warm hands all over her. She really didn't have any inhibitions about her body. He spoke softer "Just asking." "One."

"Boy or girl?"

"Girl."

"The father?" he asked. His breathing was becoming heavier with every answer. He couldn't wait to hold her. Her voice was captivating him.

"History."

"And the mother?" He spoke desperately bursting with desire. The only response she could breath before they reached out to each other was...

"Yours."

He grabbed her closely to him. They stood kissing in the moonlight. As they lay down on the bed, he continued to kiss her all over. She desperately needed what he was offering. She fell in love with his touch. She greedily accepted his kisses as they spent what felt like hours locked together. They lay in each other's arms, staring into the ceiling, each with their own thoughts.

He had been around, but after spending hours with this young woman he realized he wanted to be the one to take her wherever she wanted to go. He wanted desperately to rescue her from whatever demons she held on to. Not knowing his intentions, Trace was planning in her own mind that she was going to make sure that this man stuck around for a while. In her heart Trace had found what she needed. And even though she knew this couldn't possibly be right, she prayed God would bless it. The whole week had gone by with Trace completely in a blur. Her friends noticed. Everyone informed her of the smile that seemed to be painted on her face.

Trace knew it too. She couldn't believe love was happening to her so quickly. She made up her mind to do whatever it took to make Jeronn happy. Everything shy of obsession. She reminded herself to call Mikah on her break at work. It was Friday and she couldn't wait to leave to get to Mikah's house. As she was leaving she bumped into her friend DeeDee who was just coming to work. "Where have you been?" She asked.

"Nowhere." She smiled. She wasn't really able to control this smile yet. It was as if she wanted the whole world to know on one hand, but on the other hand she wanted to keep it to herself like a secret. "What are you so happy about?" she questioned further.

"I'm not that happy but I do have a lot to tell you girl. I met this guy. He is so fine."

"What guy? And where did you meet him?"

"Of all places for me to be in, I met him at a hole in the wall bar. Now don't frown like that. The brothers got it going on in every way."

"How long have you known him?" she asked. DeeDee was like the big sister that Trace never had. She was always looking out for her. She didn't want DeeDee to worry this time. Although she wasn't too happy about this line of questions. "A week." she defended.

"Aw girl, you act like you met him five minutes ago. Calm down."

"Excuse me. I'm just showing a little enthusiasm Miss. Just cause you're all married. I'm just trying to get where you are okay!!?"

"Well if he's the bomb, what he does want you for?" She teased.

"Ha Ha very funny!" Trace was hardly amused. "Just call me at the desk tonight when you get home. Or are you going over Mr. Man's house?" she asked.

"Very cute. And his name is Mr. Jeronn Clarke."

"Jeronn?" she frowned. "Anyway," she was ready to go now. "I'll call you at the desk tonight. I don't wanna miss my bus." She started walking backwards to let her know she was really leaving. She caught the bus to 69th street from downtown and stood on the bus stop waiting for the next bus. She didn't feel like catching the El today. She didn't feel like listening to rappers who wanted money in their hats when they were done with their three minutes of entertainment. Besides she couldn't get him off her mind. She did notice that he hadn't called her all week though. But no biggie. She knew already that they were meant to be. She could feel it way down inside. Standing on the bus stop, she thought of going to pick up her baby first and decided to just go to Mikah's house and pick up the baby later.

Chapter Five

"Who is it?"

"Come and see!"

"Oh is this Miss Trace? The girl who ditched me for some man she met in a bar?"

"Girl, open this door. I have to talk to you!" They were cracking up. "So what you doing tonight?"

"Girl nothing. I'm about to kill these kids."

"Well kill'em and come in the front room. I got gossip girl."

"You so crazy. Here I come let me just get them straightened out. Y'all get in here and clean up this room or I ain't cookin' for nobody." Mikah was yelling upstairs as she walked down the hall. Mikah had four of the cutest kids you ever seen. Two boys and two girls. She wasn't married but they all had the same dad. She was so down to earth and cool. There wasn't anything she couldn't relate to. "Girl you are so crazy." Trace shouted. Trace really liked having Mikah for her friend. Mikah had been around for her through the long haul. No matter what. They had talked each other through some pretty tripped out times. One for the other. Mikah was even there after Trace stopped dating Sherod. Mikah's younger brother. And when Trace went through her stage of trying real hard to be a Christian, Mikah supported her fully. Seemed proud of her even. Always encouraging her to go on. Mikah was cool. "Girl these kids can be so bad sometimes."

"One day I'm gone be doing the same thing with Chanelle," she said.

"And how is the little princess?" she asked. "She's fine. I'm going to pick her up when I leave here. You know she don't be wanting to leave her grandma house."

"So what happened to you and that fine fool you left with at the club? What's his name again?"

"Jeronn. And we had a good time honey. First he took me to breakfast and then he took me to dessert!"

"AAAHHHHH!!!" They screamed in goofy harmony. "And girl, he make love like he made it up!! Mph! He was so smooth. It was like in a love novel girl. Heavy breathing and all." "Sounds to me like he put it on you. Was it that good girl?"

"MMM-hmmm..mmm hmmm." She hummed like the song on the 'Jefferson's'.

"Well be careful. Make sure he doesn't have a wife or a girlfriend stashed somewhere. I mean if it looks good, walks good, talks good, got a job and a car and his own money, believe me honey, he ain't walking alone. You better believe that."

"Well when we went to breakfast I asked him and he said he does have someone he's been seeing off and on." Mikah gave Trace her *I know you told him to step to the curb* look.

"Wait a minute though before you say anything Mick. I'm not hearing that. The man is mine and gone be mine!! You wait and see." Mikah had to watch out for her friend. Trace could be real gullible sometimes. She meant well, but she needed steering here and there.

"Well where is he now?"

"I don't know. But he lives right down the street from you."

"What? Where? I've never seen him before."

"On Oakley."

"Whhaatt? For real??" She dragged. "Why haven't you talked to him?"

"He hasn't called me and I haven't called him." "Why not?"

"I don't know. I don't want to seem pushy."

"What are you talkin' about seem pushy?"

"I don't know Mick. Something about him intimidates me."

"Girl please! We gone walk down there right now." Trace's stomach fluttered with excited butterflies. "Girl I don't want to walk down there. He'll think I'm a stalker or something," she laughed. "Honey please. You done already slept with the man. A knock on his door ain't gone kill him. Now come on. Y'all better have the room cleaned before I come back. I'll be back in ten minutes. Come on Trace and don't make me drag you cause you know I will." They laughed. Mikah was her girl.

"Ok Trace," they started walking. "If his woman there we'll throw her out." They laughed harder. She felt better. They walked down the street.

"His woman doesn't live around here." "Oh yeah, where does she live?" "Jeronn said she lives in another state. In Wisconsin. And he goes to see her on weekends so he might not even be here." "Well that's what we're going to see. Now speed up."

"Mikah you knock on the door." Mikah sighed and knocked.

"Yes who is it?"

"Hi..Um, is Jeronn home?" Trace managed to say. The door opened.

"He's upstairs in the attic baby. Go on up." It was an older lady who came to the door. Must have been his grandmother she thought. "Come in." Trace turned to Mikah.

"No." she whispered back. "Just come down to my house when you leave." Trace gave her an *I'm gonna kill you* look.

"I have to go feed my kids girl. Now go on." Trace smiled. "Bye and you know I'm gonna get you right?" She said before closing the door with a goofy smile. She was dreading every step and wishing Mikah was beside her. She got so nervous she almost turned around to leave. "No," Mikah whispered. She smacked her lips. She walked past the living room and up the stairs to the attic. As she made it to the top of the stairs, she heard some instruments playing around and loud talking. She knocked on the door. "Grandma, I'm rehearsing right now, whoever it is take a message." She knocked again, giggling inside. "Grandma, not right now okay?" She waited a minute before knocking again.

"Yes Grandma!" she could tell his voice was becoming agitated. "It's not Grandma."

"Well who is it then?" he opened the door. When he saw her face he smiled. Jeronn's smile made her tingle all over her back. Goodness he was gorgeous she thought. "Hey girl. What's up? What you doing here?"

"Nothing. Just thought I'd stop by." She smiled back at him. They held each other's gaze before Jeronn said, "Let me introduce you to everyone. Everyone, This is Trace. The finest black queen on the south side of Chicago." Trace blushed and smiled her sexiest smile while the guys looked. "Trace this Ty, this is Twayne a.k.a. lazy ass." Everyone laughed. And this is Denver and he's just hangin' out." He said with a wave of his hand. They laughed again. "No I'm kidding. These are my boys and this is our group."

"Group? As in band?"

"Uh no, not really. More like a rap group?"

"Oh rap. You didn't seem like a rapper type when we met."

"Well I mess around a little." he said offhanded. He cleared his throat.

"Well," Denver was the first to speak, "I guess we better get going man. Uh Trace it was very nice to meet you and have a good night."

"Man don't be trying to act all like a gentleman, just get out." Jeronn joked.

"Aw man, it's a lady in the room and you know me and the ladies."

"Yeah I do and she's here to see me not u so disappear dude and I'll hook up with you later." "Aw man, don't trip. I'll get up with you."

"See ya Twayne, bye Ty." They all seemed a little too couth to be rappers she thought.

"I didn't mean to break up your meeting Jeronn. I'd be more than happy to come back another time."

"No baby you alright. I'm sure Jeronn wants us to leave anyway now that you're here. Hey man, ain't she the one you said can sing?" Ty asked.

"Yeah, Maybe you'd like to sing for us sometime. How about now?"

"Oh no I couldn't really. I don't sing well in front of people."

"Yes you do. You sang well at the club."

"Yeah but I was also too drunk to really care," she said nervously. She was hoping they wouldn't push this. She was nervous enough and her stomach was bubbling with butterflies. "Just a little," Ty said.

"Come on. Sing to this tape." He popped the tape in and it played the coolest funky rap. "What should I sing?"

"Twayne handed her some lyrics" She nodded her head to the track and sang the words on the sheets. She had a really good vibe going. They were all nodding in agreement. She was nervous. Her laughter broke the tension and they all started talking.

"Alright man, that's it. You heard her. So I'll get up with yall later alright?"

"Cool man." Denver said. After they gave dap they turned to leave.

"Trace I'm gonna walk them downstairs, can I get you anything?" "Oh no I'm good, thanks."

Trace sat on the bed waiting for Jeronn to come back. She noticed a picture of a girl holding a little girl on the mirror. She looked closer and became a little jealous. The girl wasn't that pretty but she wasn't unattractive either. She almost felt guilty for being there. She straightened up when she heard Jeronn coming back.

"Beautiful, sexy and talented. What does a man do to deserve such wealth?"

Trace smiled.

"Is something wrong? I'm sorry he put you on the spot like that, but you do sing good girl."

"Thank you. So that's your music huh?"

"Yeah," Jeronn said. "Did you like it?"

"Yeah, you're talented too."

"Thanks," said Jeronn. Silence filled the room. "So who have I got in this room with me --the shy girl I thought I kissed away or the vivacious woman who tried to tear me alive huh?" Trace laughed. "Neither."

"Then what seems to be the problem Miss? What you thinking under that pretty black hair of yours?"

She couldn't get over how cute his little lips were. "Listen? I realize that I don't know you that well, but I think I can be real with you can't I?"

"Uh oh. Sure what's on your mind?" He stooped between her knees.

"Well it's just that I never expected a nice looking brother like you to have jungle fever. I mean I take something like that as a slap in the face personally." He looked confused.

"Not only that, you have a mixed child too?"

"Wait a minute. How do you know all this?" She felt stupid and hated to be nosy but she pointed to the picture. He stared at it like he'd never seen it before.

"Well would you say something?" she asked.

"I mean you really don't owe me any explanations but could you explain to me how brothers like yourself get jungle fever?"

"First of all," he spoke matter of fact. "I don't have jungle fever and she's not white and that's not my child."

"Oops! Well she looks white and .." "And don't think about that." he jumped in. "Listen..I..That's my girlfriend. I did tell you about her. That's her daughter. "Though I do have two children of my own. A daughter and a son."

"Are you still involved with their mom?"

"Actually," he exhaled. "It's mom's." She waited. He chuckled.

"I guess this is where we get to know each other more huh?" he asked. She smiled.

"I guess so. But that depends on how far you go and how much you want to tell me."

"Well let's see. My son is the oldest. He and his mom are in Ohio. My daughter and her mom live some damned where. They always moving. I only really talk to the kids over the phone. Never to their moms if I don't have to. The only way I'm involved with their moms is through child support. Is that cool?"

"Well I guess it has to be."

"Why?"

"If I want to be around you then I guess it has to be." He pulled her hand to his.

"No it doesn't have to be cool. If you have a problem you let me know. I'm only several years older than you, but I been around enough to know how to make things work a little better for myself and anyone involved with me. Does that sound fair?"

"Yes. Thanks." This man is too good to be true. Where does he come up with this stuff? She felt a new confidence. This man was not full of bull and that meant a whole lot to her. She was impressed.

"No thanks sweetheart. I do love my African American sisters. Especially ones as sweet and chocolate as you are." If she was light skinned her face would be beet red. "So what are you doing tonight?"

"Nothing, tired. I need a break." He turned on the TV. "Why are you all dressed up?" "I'm not I just got off work." "You hungry?" he asked. "No not really." They sat watching TV for a while. Actually he watched and Trace watched him. He caught her staring and he stared back. Right into her eyes. He reached for her hand. He knew what she wanted and she knew it too. The way he looked at her made every part of her come to life. She ached to feel him inside her. His thickness. His weight. She wanted it all. She wanted to feel the heat of his body pressing against her own making everything else disappear. She wondered herself how this man could have a woman somewhere else and still light this fire inside her. It was like the thought of him relit the flame over and over and she wanted him desperately. It felt like they'd had been lovers forever. They knew

each other instinctively. He turned to look at the TV. She turned it off.

He looked at her again. She looked at him. She had never been the

aggressor, but she wasn't about to start now. He reached to her with

passion. She felt like screaming. His touch, his smell, his look, it all felt

so right. He laid her down and looked at her. His eyes were so beautiful.

She wondered what he was thinking. He stopped and leaned up. He went

into the drawer and pulled out something small. At first she assumed it

might be a condom but they didn't use one the first time so she waited. He

pulled out his lighter and lit it. It was a joint. She felt a little

uncomfortable. She'd never ever smoked a joint and never even thought

about it. She also had no desire to do it now. It's crazy, but all of a

sudden in her mind, drugs were in the room. She didn't know what to do.

She turned the TV back on. "So you don't get high huh?"

"No I don't. I don't smoke at all."

"Well here just try this."

"No."

"Come on just take a puff." Ordinarily she wouldn't even consider it or

give it a thought. But for a split second it seemed all right. She'd never

done anything that bad before so she felt one time wouldn't kill her.

"I don't know how."

"I'll show you. Just take a puff, a little one, and swallow it and hold it in and let it out slowly." She tried it. Her chest was burning. She let the smoke out quickly and coughed. It burned more. She coughed so hard her eyes were watering. She thought she was going to die. She felt embarrassed. She just put her head in the pillow and coughed it out. She tried to laugh like it was funny.

"It's burning. Get me some water." He smiled at her sheepishly and went and brought her some Kool-Aid with ice. It tasted so good. She really couldn't taste it, but the fact that it was cold felt good going down. After she calmed down he sat next to her and held her hand again. "Trace, can I kiss you?" he asked.

"You don't have to ask?" He turned the TV off and the stereo on. She felt a little high but everything was all right. He turned the lights off. They could see each other from the streets lights reflecting inside the window. His body was nice and firm. She unbuttoned his shirt and he was rubbing her shoulders and caressing her neck. She placed deep, lusty kisses across his chest and let her fingers slide across his abdomen. Before long they were both undressed and admiring each other's body. She wanted him to love her. She needed him to love her that night, all over. She pulled him closer. His pale skin felt so warm. He laid her down on the bed and caressed her gently. He lay beside her. The anticipation of what he would do to her overwhelmed her senses. He made her feel like a virgin again. He kissed her softly. His hand slid across her breasts playfully teasing her nipples. He leaned forward to taste them. The fact that he had so much height and weight over her only added to his masculinity and she was overwhelmed with attraction to him. He leaned down more to kiss her stomach and her sides. It felt so good. He massaged and kissed her inner thighs and stomach. She was sensitive all over. His hand cupped her between her legs and the warmth of his large hands made her hotter than she already was. She felt a shutter when he put his lips between her legs. It felt so good. His lips were so soft. He knew exactly what to do with them too. The way he made her feel when they made love let her know that she could love this man forever. How could anyone be so strong and so gentle at the same time? She wanted to give her whole self to him and she wanted the same in return. Whatever he had to offer she wanted and whatever he needed she wanted to give. Trace knew right now that she loved this man and he was gonna be around for a while.

Chapter Six

Miami, Florida

Jeronn was back through the door by the time they were both through remembering the wonderful times they had when they met. He still loved her so much. Trace wanted so much to feel that love again. She wanted to 'be' again. She was so afraid. Afraid to let go again. Lord knows she didn't wanna get hurt again. She really couldn't take that. She stood there staring at him. *Oh God I still love him* she thought. He walked over and reached out to her. "You remember?" He asked.

"Yeah I remember Jeronn but that was a long time ago and we're not together anymore. You made that choice a long time ago. You got married remember? Jeronn just go and leave me alone." She wanted to cry so badly. She walked over to her desk and opened the drawer. She lit a joint.

"Baby please? I know things have changed, but let me make it up to you. Come on and lets go and get something to eat or something. Let's just get out of here for awhile." She walked closer to him and blew the smoke in his face. She wanted to hear these words but she hadn't trusted any man for a long time. She didn't want to get caught up in the same web. But she wanted Jeronn's words to be true. She still loved him like no other. She went in the bathroom to freshen up and get dressed. Jeronn sat on the couch while he waited. He looked around the room again. Everything in here was beautiful and soft. Just like Trace. He wanted her out of here. He couldn't understand why she was here in the first place. She had everything she could ever want. She had fame, beauty and money and a wonderful daughter. She'd become famous so fast after he left her, he was a little jealous at times. But why have this secret life? He decided the best thing to do was to get her some help. Maybe some counseling or something. What else could he do? He owed her something. He wondered if Chanelle had any idea what her mom was up to. What did she think? She had to be about sixteen or seventeen by now. He would call her first chance he got.

Trace came out dressed like she had just spent a million dollars on her clothes. She had pinned her hair up with a beautiful diamond pen. She had on a two piece lime colored jacket and skirt. She was impeccable. Her legs were long and beautiful. She smelled wonderful all the way across the room. She took his breath away. "Come on and let's go." he rose.

As they were leaving someone knocked at the door. They stood there staring at the door. Trace knew what it was. Jeronn was shocked that it was happening while he was still there. A knock again. Her heart was racing a mile a minute. "Who is it?" Trace shouted.

"I'm looking for Misty?" someone stuttered. Jeronn quickly opened the door. This was too weird. He stood looking at what he considered to be an idiot in the doorway while he controlled his anger. Under the circumstances Trace felt she had no choice but to lie about whom she was. She knew what the strange man wanted and what he was doing there. Trace quickly put on her sunglasses.

"Ain't nobody here named Misty." Jeronn offered.

"Isn't that her right there?" he pointed.

"I don't think so brother." Jeronn reasoned, stepping in his way.

"There's nobody here for you. Is there something I can help you with?" Jeronn asked.

"She looks like she's here to me. And if you through talking *brother* I'd like to come in." The man spoke while licking his big brown lips. Trace had never seen this man before. He was new. Obviously a referral. He did not look like the type of man who would go to a prostitute. He was more of a slim Bryant Gumble type brother. He wore Isi Miyake cologne. Trace could smell that scent blindfolded. She loved it. Trace spoke up before Jeronn could punch the man in the face, which she noticed he was real close to doing.

"I'm sorry sir, but I'm not who you're looking for. My name is not Misty and I believe the woman you're looking for is gone and won't be back here. So why don't you go on ahead and go?" She hoped that would satisfy the fool, but he looked very determined. How could this be happening to her? Her ex-man standing here defending her for something she shouldn't have been doing in the first damned place. The man stared, a little disappointed now. "What's going here?" he seemed desperate.

"I have money," he stated.

"It 's got nothing to do with money sir, I said the woman you want is no longer here. Would you kindly leave before I call the police?" *Yeah right.* She knew damned well she better not be calling the police. She'd be the first one they arrested.

"Hey don't I know you Miss?" the man asked. Trace tilted her head down like she'd been doing for years many times before when people thought they'd recognized her.

"Honey?" She gave Jeronn the eye letting him know that this was enough.

"Look man," Jeronn reasoned, "You don't know my wife and she don't know you so now just leave before it gets really ugly out here. I don't know who you're looking for, but there's nothing here for you. My wife and I are on our way out so if you'll excuse us?" The man stood looking around the halls like maybe he had the wrong apartment after all. *No he didn't call me his wife* she thought.

"Okay then, I'm going. No need to get hoss-style my brotha. But I know I know you lady. I'm not crazy."

"This is your last warning fool. Walk away from here." He threatened. It was almost funny. He sounded like James Evans on Good Times. The man left. Trace was so ashamed and afraid that the man actually may have recognized her. She was also ashamed that Jeronn saw the type of men that she sometimes had to deal with. Although a lot of them were highly paid square dudes who couldn't get anyone to sleep with them, they weren't highly paid enough that they could buy it from even the most desperate of women. Sometimes she did get a sleaze ball or two. She would look through the security hole and if they didn't look clean cut; she definitely wasn't going to let them in.

After this incident, Trace made up her mind that Jeronn would never see her in this position again. It was way too embarrassing. They made their way down to his car, opting to leave hers in the underground parking. Life sure is funny. Many times she had thought about ending it all but the love her sweet Chanelle gives her also gave her hope. Trace turned to Jeronn and wondered what he was thinking. What he thought about her now. She still didn't know what was going on in his life. Had to be something or he wouldn't be visiting a prostitute.

"Maybe I better get home. I have an early start in the morning. I have a photo shoot for my next album. Have you heard? It's coming out soon."

"Yes, actually I had heard. It's gonna be the 'Trace Reese Greatest Hits' album right?" "Yeah. I thought it was a bit too soon for it but my manager says, I have enough going on out there that I could put something together like this and get away with it." She sounded very business like all of a sudden. Even to herself. *I got my nerve!* She thought.

"Jeronn?" she started. He cut off her conversation. "Not now alright? I know what you're gonna ask but I'm not ready to talk about it just yet. And right now you seem to be more important to me." He put his hand on her knee. "Trace whatever you want, I'm here for you." Jeronn knew he was saying the right things. He knew he was what was best for Trace. He decided to put his own troubles aside for now because he knew once he made Trace okay he would be okay too. "Where are we going?" she asked.

"I thought we'd go to my home if that's okay."

"Hell naw it's not okay!" she yelled. "You stop this car right now."

"Trace it's not what you think. Retha's not there anymore. We'll be alone." She took a sharp breath. "I'm sorry Jeronn. I just have a problem

62

with trusting people is all. I'm sorry. I know you wouldn't do me like that." "Baby it's okay. You just lay back and relax." Trace lay back in the soft leather seats looking up at the grey sky. She prayed silently. *Lord please take me out of this hell. Now that Jeronn's here I know you'll make it all right. I know you didn't let him show up for nothing.* Trace felt really tired. I need sleep she thought. She was coming down from her high and getting hungry. She closed her eyes and soaked in the peace. Jeronn was rescuing her. Again he was her knight and shining armor. Where would this take her she wondered? Would life be beautiful again? She thought it might but she sensed trouble. Jeronn didn't seem at all like the same man. He seemed nice but withdrawn. She wondered what was going on with him after all these years. As they drove she noticed a big billboard with her face and name on it.

"Egyptian Glow. The make up fit for a queen." Trace said. "I remember the first time I saw that commercial." Jeronn said. "I couldn't believe you were doing make up commercials on top of everything else. I was so excited for you."

"Please. You have to water that stuff down just to even it out. But you didn't hear that from me." They laughed. "Every time I wore that make up, it felt like I was putting on a mask. I don't even wear that crap," she continued.

"Yeah, I was very happy for you when I saw that commercial." Jeronn repeated. Trace looked over at Jeronn sensing his turmoil. "Jeronn listen,"

"Trace," he interrupted. "That's a real long story and I'm not ready to discuss it now."

"Well how are you gonna help me if you can't help yourself? You know my dirty secret and now I wanna know yours." He frowned as if to be exhausted. He was not ready for this at all. "Are you hungry?"

"I hadn't thought about it but I think I am. Shoot I've been so high I haven't even thought about food. Hell in between men and hiding my identity all the time I just bathe and sit around watching TV and.."

"Alright, alright..I get the picture," he interrupted. He wasn't prepared to hear all that. *Damn, who did she think she was talking to anyway?* "I don't want to hear about that. I'm sorry but that's gonna have to be a topic we discuss with a therapist. Not with each other. If you absolutely have to talk about it, I hope it can wait till tomorrow when we can go to a professional and we'll start getting some help." Trace's first instinct was to argue, but then thought better of it.

"Maybe you're right Jeronn. I'm sure you know what's best. But how do you know I can trust a therapist. My face will be in the papers the next day!!" She was feeling aggravated now.

"No Trace, I don't know what's best. I'm just as lost as you and I'm sorry for speaking to you that way. I only want to help as much as I can baby. But I can't hear about this just now okay?"

"Okay Jeronn. I'm sorry too." She spoke softly. He sighed.

"So pretty lady, where do you want to eat?"

"MMM" she pondered..."How about your house? Are you still a master chef?"

"Oh the best baby, no doubt. You know how I do it. You about to get some of the best master cheffing in the world."

"Cheffing?? Oh my goodness Jeronn where'd you find that word?"

"What??" they laughed. Feeling a little more hopeful. Trace finally relaxed.

"It's almost 8 o clock." Chanelle was talking to her dad on the phone long distance from Chicago. "Where could she be dad? I'm getting worried and Mama Sue hasn't heard from her all day." Chanelle listened to her father trying to comfort her but that didn't work. Chanelle was worried about her mom. She'd been acting more strangely for the past year and she wasn't used to it. "Well okay Dad I'm gonna go now. I have more calls to make. I love you too bye." Chanelle sat back and sighed deeply. Ever since she decided to go to a local college, she noticed things were strange at home.

When she was away everything seemed fine. But now that she's home more often to look after her mom she noticed her mom is just not the same. She had no clue as to why her mom acts the way she does. But she really hadn't noticed until she decided to go to school in Florida instead of going away which was her original plan. "Mama Sue!!" She yelled down the stairs. "Don't cook dinner for me. I have a feeling mommy won't be home tonight."

"Okay sweetie. You go out and have some fun. Okay? Stop worrying about your mama. She can take care of herself."

"I know Mama Sue. I just miss having her around so much. Something's not right and I don't know what it is." "Don't worry Chanelle. She'll be home soon. You worry about yourself and start thinking about yourself a little more. Yes?"

"Sure Mama Sue. Thanks for listening." She smiled at her.

"No problem now. You go out and have fun okay?"

"Thanks Mama Sue. I'm just gonna go up to my room. If mommy calls get me okay?" "Okay Missy." Chanelle appreciated Mama Sue a whole lot. She had been around ever since mommy and Jeronn had split up. She was only a child when he left but she remembered clearly the way things happened.

"Mama Sue had explained to her that mommy was not feeling well and needed a little time by herself. Mama Sue would make sure Chanelle went to school and ate and was well taken care of. She was more than a nanny or a housekeeper. She was like a second mother. She even scolded her when the time was right. She was the prettiest Asian lady Chanelle had ever seen. Although, when she was little girl she didn't know she was Asian. She just knew she was pretty. She had a beautiful name that Chanelle had a hard time pronouncing when she was little so it turned into Mama Sue over the years. And Maja Sul Li didn't seem to mind at all. Now that Chanelle was older, Mama Sue became more of a close friend than anything else. They talked about everything together and she was glad Mama Sue was there. As Chanelle lay in her bed thinking, she remembered when all the problems started. She remembered when mommy cried all the time and she remembered when Jeronn left. Jeronn had found another star.

Chapter Seven

Chicago, IL

"Oh I can't believe it." "Me either baby. We finally did it." Jeronn and Trace were sitting down to dinner when the phone call came that their record deal was finally going through and that an additional solo contract with Trace for an R and B career was happening just the way they wanted. "Trace, you know they want us to move right?"

"Move? Where?"

"To Florida baby. That's where the studios are. We'll be cool baby and don't give me that look. Believe me it's long overdue." Trace leaned over and gave a great big kiss to Chanelle. "You hear that little mama. Mommy's gonna be rich, and so are you!! Hey, Hey! Go head! Go head! Go head!" She danced around the room.

"Rich. Wow. For real mommy? Wait till I tell all my friends."

"Noo baby, not yet. Let's not tell anybody yet okay? It's gonna be our family secret okay baby?"

"Okay mommy." Trace was so happy she could scream. "Well Jeronn, baby, maybe we can now talk about or at least think about getting married now?"

"Baby when this deal goes through you can have anything you want?"

"Yeah, that sounds cool but sweetie do you want to?"

"Of course. Now that we got a lil' change we can do it all."

"Me too mommy right?" squealed little Chanelle, not wanting to be left out of the conversation. "You too, mama's wittle baby." She smothered her with baby talk and kisses. They were so happy, they were gonna be paid and still in love. Trace loved her little family.

After moving to Florida finally, they couldn't believe how big their new house was. It was white on the outside with lots of windows. The trees were trimmed ever so precise. The grass was so green you wanted to dive into it. The birds were chirping. The air was clean. It looked like a small castle. Everything was immaculate, just the way Trace had imagined it to be. She had no problem with leaving Chicago behind her at all. In her mind this was her dream and it was definitely where she belonged. It took no time for Trace to get settled. She became very content. Chanelle started her new school and everything was going along fine. Trace believed that they were one big happy family. That was until Jeronn began to change. He was always gone taking care of one thing or another. According to Jeronn, Trace's contract wasn't in the works yet. They were only interested in his music ability for the moment but that she would be getting in the studio soon. She bide her time decorating the house and exploring all the rooms and creating ideas about what to do in them.

Shopping became her favorite pastime. Especially shopping without looking at the price tags. She was getting her hair done regularly. Which was definitely a plus in the looks department. This was the life for Trace. What could be better?

Trace eventually became aware that she couldn't manage the big house alone. She spoke to Jeronn about a housekeeper and someone to help with Chanelle when she starts going into the studio. Besides, she thought, isn't that how all the rich folks do it anyway? Jeronn thought the idea was okay and began asking around from people he knew. Maja Sul came along and quickly became part of the family. Trace felt a little guilty at the idea of needing help. She considered herself the model strong black woman who didn't need anyone's help, but now that she could afford it she thought a little help wouldn't hurt. One night, Trace thought she'd surprise Jeronn with a romantic night at home. She had prepared a dinner for two to take place in their room on their private balcony. She took extra care getting dressed. She had bought sexy lingerie she wanted to wear for her night with her man. She bought new perfume, new underwear, new everything for this night. It was no special occasion. Except for being happy to be here and not where they used to be. He had been spending a lot of time at the studio, but he had told her this morning that he should be home this evening with no problem. She stood looking in the mirror, placing her new diamond earrings in her ear smiling to herself at how in love she was. There was a knock at the door. She assumed it was Chanelle getting ready for bed and come to kiss her night-night.

"Miss Trace, Mister Jeronn called and said he's not going to make it home tonight for dinner and you eat without him." She delivered with her ever so ready to please smile. She knew Trace was hurt, but what could she do? It's not her place to sit and talk with her boss. No matter how much she wanted to help. "Thank you Maja. Uh just put Chanelle to bed for me please. I'm not very hungry."

"Yes Miss," she smiled pleasantly and walked away. Jeronn hadn't been making it for dinner quite a lot over the past few months. Trace thought he must be very busy at work. She decided to call him and see how he was. Sitting down on the bed to dial, she felt a sharp pain in her stomach. She had been having that pain for two days now and didn't know why this one hit her so hard. She couldn't move at all. "Oh God!" she screamed. "What is this?"

She rose slowly and made her way to the bathroom. She put some cold water on her face to try to cool down the sweating. She walked back to the bed. "Maja!" she yelled.

"Yes Miss?" she answered already coming up the stairs. "Maja call Mr. Clark and tell him to meet me at the hospital."

"Yes Miss. You need an ambulance?" "No I'll drive. Is Chanelle in bed?" "Yes Miss. I'll call Mr. Clark for you now." "Thank you Maja." Trace walked down the stairs like a woman in labor. But she couldn't help it. It hurt like hell. She slowly walked to her car. "Miss Trace, he says he'll go there now." She yelled behind her. "Okay Maja. Thank you. And please watch my baby." She was breathing heavily. She felt like her insides were had been stabbed or something. The pain was so sharp. Trace drove slowly but she finally made it. Jeronn was already there. He met her at her car. "Baby, what's up? What happened?"

"I don't know, but it hurts." She felt the tears about to fall just hearing him ask her what's wrong. "Well come in here I've already got you signed in." "Not so fast Jeronn it hurts."

"Okay. Okay. What were you doing?"

"I was waiting for you to come home."

"Ok well sit in this wheelchair and I'll take care of everything." "Thanks Jeronn." She looked up at him. Trying to read any sign of guilt in his face. Momentarily she contemplated the idea that he might have burned her or gave her some nasty STD. But right now he was her savior. He seemed to be there for her when she needed him the most. "I'm sorry I called you away from work sweetie. I know you were busy." He looked at her and turned his head. "Don't worry about that baby. This is more important." He didn't look her in the eyes, as was his usual way. Trace noticed that and she wanted to know why. But now was not the time.

She felt like screaming bloody murder. She got in to see the doctor and after a few tests and some poking, he told her what the problem was. "Mr. and Mrs. Reese, the pain you're having is due to dead tissue that is still lining your uterus."

"Huh?" they asked in unison. "How did it get there?"

"Well Miss Reese it's seems you were having a miscarriage." They both looked in shock. "You didn't know you were pregnant?" The doctor asked. "No. I didn't." She had been so worried about other things she completely forgot all about having a period.

"I'll leave you two to talk for a moment and a nurse will be right in to prep you for removal. It's a simple procedure. I've done it before. It's a little painful but we will try to alleviate that as much as possible. You'll be uncomfortable for a few days. After about an hour of rest you can go home with some antibiotics and you should feel like your old self again in no time." He smiled reassuringly. "Thank you doctor. Thank you so much." Trace started to cry. "Trace, don't cry." He tried to be comforting. But he wasn't succeeding at all.

"What do you mean don't cry. I feel like God is punishing me." *'Here we go'* he thought. "Why would you say something like that?" he was getting upset now. He knew what she was going say before she even said it. "Jeronn, I don't mean to bring this up again, but we've been together for a few years now and we're still not married. I know I don't say this but it's starting to bother me. I always know I'm living in sin. I want to change that before it's too late Jeronn. God has been blessing us with so many good things and we're just taking advantage. But way down deep I know something has got to change. I know it's wrong. And you do too." Jeronn did not feel like hearing this right now. He sighed. Instead of telling her what he was really feeling, he was going to have to pacify her as usual. He was feeling guilty about not being man enough to tell her what's really going on in his life. He knew brothers always talk about how they'd let a woman know if he's been cheating but it always seemed easier said than done. He felt like a chump for not confessing to what was going on. He didn't really quite know himself. He'd loved her since the night they met. He wanted to always be there for her. But how could he tell her what was going on with him, when he didn't really understand it himself? Plus, isn't there a code that men live by? I mean, if she doesn't know it shouldn't hurt her. She wasn't letting this marriage thing go. And why did she have to bring God into it all the time? She likes to pull out the

74

guilt knife and it's not deep enough until she spits a little God on the blade. Dang. They drove home from the hospital in silence. Eventually, she fell asleep from the effects of the drugs the doctor gave her. When they arrived home, Jeronn did whatever he could to make her feel comfortable. He didn't want to talk so he satiated her by holding her until she fell back to sleep. He felt her hot tears on his hand before she drifted off. He knew she was feeling bad, but he didn't say a word.

"Wake up sleepy head." Trace stretched like a lazy cat. "Ow!!" She opened her eyes as wide as golf balls. "Whoa hold still. Take it easy."

"Oh Jeronn. Where am I?"

"At home woman. Don't you recognize your own room?"

"This isn't my room. This is the guest room and when did I get in here?"

"Last night. Really late. I had Maja fix up the room and make it comfortable for you. How do you like it?"

"I like my own room better. Why didn't you just sleep in the guest room? I want to sleep in my own bed from now on."

"Well I didn't want to hurt you in our bed. And I needed our bed. This bed is too soft for my back. I thought you'd appreciate it. Here I made you breakfast and cut some fresh flowers with my own two hands."

"Wow Jeronn what's the occasion for all this attention?" "Now you know nothing's too good for my baby. Besides I just thought I'd make my beautiful black queen a meal fit for a queen." She sipped her coffee looking at him through squinted eyes. He was up to something. "That's sweet of you. You've thought of everything. Except this room thing. I'm not sleeping in here." She ate heartily.

"So, what's the matter with you? You don't want to sleep with me or something?"

"Here you go. That's not it Trace." He sighed. "It's just that the doctor told me that we couldn't...you know."

"What? So what? That don't mean we can't sleep together. What's really going on Jeronn? I want you to tell me now. Is it about me bringing up marriage again? Because if it is Jeronn, I do believe it's time we talked. I mean we have mostly everything we want and now there should be nothing standing in our way. Baby all I want do is set a date ok?"

"Trace we need to talk about this okay, but not now. When you are better."

"No, Now." She demanded. "I'm tired of waiting and I want to talk now."

"Boy you don't seem like you're in much pain."

"I'm a big girl and don't change the subject. Do you still love me Jeronn?" She had to ask. "Of course Trace. That will never change."

"Then what has changed Jeronn?" She sat up more in bed pushing the tray aside. "Why don't you come home at night anymore? I know you're working hard, but something else is happening and you know it."

"Trace now is not the time." "Yes it is Jeronn. Is there something you need to tell me? If you don't talk to me now I'll move out of this big house and find a small little apartment like we had in Chicago. There's no one to share this house with anymore. You're never home." "You have Chanelle." "Don't go there Jeronn. Don't ever use my baby's name in my face like that. Ever? You got that? Why are you acting like this Jeronn?" She felt exasperated. "Jeronn," she sighed, "you're starting to piss me off okay? I sit around here all day taking care of whatever you want taken care of and you can't even talk to me okay? You come home sometimes and you want your back rubbed, your feet rubbed, you head massaged, your dick sucked and your ass kissed and you can't open up to me a little when I want you to?"

He breathed in deeply. He wasn't ready to talk to her right now about this, but he could see that she was about to get ready for one of her sister girl, head snapping tirades and he wasn't in the mood for it.

"Trace, we've been out here for six months now and in that time we've met a lot of people." "So?" "Wait let me finish okay? Trace you know I love you." *Exactly where is he going with this?* She thought. She held her hand up. "I know good and damn well you're not about to come to me about some other woman crap." She could tell in his eyes that that's exactly where he was going. "I don't know really what I feel. It's just that she seemed so innocent and vulnerable and I just felt like I had to help her. She actually reminds me a lot..." She held her hand up. "Baby, I'm so sorry Trace. I don't know what I can say."

Trace couldn't hold back the tears anymore. She couldn't believe what she was hearing. The more he talked the sicker she felt. "Shut up Jeronn. I don't want to hear this shit!" She was clenching her teeth so hard a headache started in the back of her head. Softly she said "Now you listen to me Mr. Jeronn Clarke. I want you to pack all of your bags right down to your damned toothbrush and get the hell out of here. I don't need you Jeronn. I have a career too. It came from your help but it's my career nonetheless. I will take care of myself and my child from now on. You are no longer welcome here. WE have nothing else to say to each other so get your sorry ass out of my face!" Her head was pounding now.

She had just told the only man she ever truly loved to leave and never come back. But hell he deserved it. "I refuse to cry," she repeated to herself. He came back in the room.

"Trace baby, at least let me stay and make sure you're alright. You just lost our baby for goodness sake." That did it. She began to yell at the top of her lungs. She threw the breakfast tray and roses across the room. The pillows from the bed also made flight. "You lousy son of a bitch! Get the fuck out of my house. Go find your innocent little vulnerable bitch and take care of *her*. Don't you ever come here again!" "Trace," he shouted back. "You can't just expect me not to see you and Chanelle ever again." "Wanna bet? I didn't expect your black ass to screw somebody else either, but you did that didn't you? Isn't that what you said?"

"I love you baby don't do this to us."

"You did it Negro. Not me. And I don't believe you just said that. I also don't believe that I asked a man like you to marry me. You ain't shit." The tears streamed down her face. Now that she was crying she couldn't stop. Her stomach was cramping and she felt dizzy from standing up so fast. "You have wasted too many years of my life you bastard. You promised me and promised me. But not anymore. When I come out of this bathroom I want you gone Jeronn. And don't look back cause I damned sure won't." "Trace." he tried to reach for her. Not just for her but for him. What had he done? He realized at this moment that he subconsciously depended on her. Depended on the knowledge that she would always be there. But now he could see her pain. Pain that he had caused emotionally and physically. At that moment he didn't want anyone else but Trace. He wished he could take back everything he had told her and just solve the problem himself. But now that she knew she would never let him take it back. He didn't know if he should even take the chance he was just given or try to win Trace back. He knew that if he tried real hard she would change her mind, but that wouldn't be fair to her and she may never trust him again. He stood in the doorway of the bathroom and looked at her standing over the sink. She was sick all over and it was all because of him. He knew that. He wanted to say he was sorry but saying it would only anger her more. All he could say was "Give Chanelle a big hug and kiss for me and Trace if you need anything." She stopped crying to face him squarely and slammed the door in his face. He left. What else could he say to her? He felt confused. He took all he could and left. Trace stood over the staircase looking out the window watching him drive away out of her life to his other woman just like that. She hurt. She hurt so badly. She felt like she was in a horrible love story.

Later that night Chanelle asked her, "Mommy when is Jeronn coming back home?" "Chanelle, Jeronn's not coming back. Um, he's got a new house that he liked and he thought he would like to live in that one instead of this one." She lied. She couldn't think of anything else. She had been thinking all day about what she could say and couldn't find anything to say. She felt guilty about wanting Chanelle to be pissed at him too. But that would be wrong. "Well why don't we go live at the new house too mommy?"

"Because Mommy likes this house and I want to live here. Don't you like this house baby?" "Yes mommy, but I want to see the new house. I want Jeronn." "I know sweetie, but you will see him again. Just not now okay? Now go finish your dinner and let Mama Sue take you up for a bath."

"Can I have some cookies?" "You can have one cookie, but you have to brush your teeth after. " "Okay but gimme a kiss mommy." She wrapped her skinny little arms around her mom and squeezed real hard. Trace remembered Jeronn's words and gave her a big hug and a kiss. It was all she could do to keep from crying again. "That was a good one mommy," they laughed. "Yes it was baby. You have the best hugs in the world." "You do too. "Sul can you clean her up please and I'll be up there in a minute?" "Yes Miss. Is there anything I can do for you?"

"No Sul but thank you. I just need some peace and quiet." She tried to sound happy but the strain in her voice gave her away. I'll be in the family room and I don't want any calls."

"Yes Miss." Chanelle had already run off for her cookie. As she reached the den the phone rang. *Please let it be him.* She thought to herself. "One moment please." she heard Sul. "Miss," she whispered "It's Mr. Clark. Do you want to talk to him?" She was torn between her love for him and his

betrayal of her trust. She had so many questions she wanted to ask though.

"I'll take it in the family room."

"Yes Miss. Good night."

"Hello Jeronn." "Trace, I miss you so much." She swallowed hard. Her

heart ached. She loved him so much. *Be strong girl.* "That's not fair

Jeronn. Don't play games with me." "Trace why does it have to be this

way? I need you. I don't want Retha. I want you. I know that now." "Oh

that's her name? Retha? What an innocent and vulnerable name." "Trace,"

he sighed in the phone. "Don't keep saying those words. You make me

sorry I said them. Please, can't we just start over?" "No Jeronn if you

cared enough to let me know how you feel about this woman then I have

to be a big girl and let you experience whatever it is you need to

experience. Jeronn I love you and you know I do, but since you've done

this to me then I have to see if I can do this on my own? How could you

do this to me? You know the type of woman I am. You could have told

me a long time ago. But you kept making promises. I've been thinking

about this all day and I can't let this stop me. I plan to go much further

than a big house and a housekeeper. I have bigger plans and I know I will

make it. You put me on the backburner for so long and now I have to do my thing. Heartache is not on the agenda." It hurt her to say these words but she had to do it. She had to let go and try. "Bye Jeronn." "Trace." "Bye Jeronn." "I love you." It was too late. She had already hung up. She didn't hear his last plea of love. She didn't hear his last goodbye.

Florida

Present Day

"Miss the phone ringing." Chanelle turned over, wondering when did she fall asleep. "Miss the phone is ringing. Maybe it's your mother calling. You want me to answer your phone?" "No Maja" she yelled back. "I'll get it." She wiped the drool that from her mouth. Good grief, she thought. "Hello?"

"Chanelle?" It was a male voice but she didn't recognize it. "Yes who is this?"

"Chanelle It's Jeronn." "Jeronn!" she said excited. "Really? How are you?"

"I'm fine" He smiled. Happy to hear her voice. "Listen Chanelle, I ran into your mom earlier today and she's here with me." "Really? What's going on? Is she okay?"

"Yeah, yeah she's fine. We bumped into each other today and kind of hung out all day and well she's a little tired. We had a big dinner. I wanted to tell you she'd be staying here tonight."

"Here where? Where are you?"

"At my home. But I'll bring her home in the morning." "Well can I speak to her? I've been so worried." "She's sleeping now. I can wake her if you want." She thought about it. "No, I'll just see you in the morning."

"Chanelle?" "Yes?"

"You're mom is going through some pretty rough changes right now and if I know her she probably hasn't discussed them with you, but when she's ready she will. And I'm just asking when she comes home in the morning kind of take it easy with the questions okay? I feel like I have no right to suggest what is best for your mom to you, seeing as how you haven't seen me in over fifteen years. I mean you gotta be about 21, 22 now right?" "Jeronn, it's cool. I understand. Listen, can I ask you a question?"

"Sure." he replied. "Where exactly did you bump into mommy at?" "Chanelle," he sighed, "tomorrow is a better time to talk. Everything will be cleared up for you. Until then, it's pretty late. You get some rest and I'll see you in the morning before noon." "Jeronn? Are you and mommy getting back together?" She hoped. As she had been hoping for so many years. "I don't know, but it's certainly nice to know you might be rooting for us. Wow, you sure sound like a mature young lady." "Thank you. It's nice to talk to you Jeronn and thanks for calling me. I'll see you tomorrow." "Ok then. Get some rest now." "I will. Bye." It certainly was nice to hear from Jeronn after all this time. She kept up with his comings and going in the tabloids ever since she was thirteen and discovered his face on the front cover of a magazine. She looked at the pictures and recognized him immediately. Although it had been a few years since she had heard anything about him. She looked at pictures of his wife LoRetha. She was very pretty. But no one compared to her mommy. Lately she had heard that they were no longer together but no one really knew. When people began to see less and less of them it confirmed it. At first he was an immediately successful producer. He was the toast of the town. And she was right by his side all the way. But something was happening between them that even the tabloids couldn't find out. Chanelle could sleep peacefully now. At least she knew her mommy was ok. She rolled over and closed her eyes half sleeping and half wondering, how her mommy ended up at Jeronn's house.

Jeronn couldn't sleep. He had Trace on his mind and in his house and he didn't want to lose her. Not this time. He looked around the big empty home. It all looked different with Retha gone. She took practically everything. Deep down he hoped things could be all right between he and Trace again. The look in her eyes made him believe he had a chance, but the fear in her heart also showed him he might not have a chance and if he did he would definitely have to go slow. But there wasn't time for slow. He needed Trace and he needed her now. He lay back on the leather sofa. It was deep and comforting. Lately all he had was that sofa to keep him warm at night. The sofa and a bottle of whatever there was to drink in the house. Retha had even taken all the liquor when she left. She was a true ghetto rat. Including his collection of fine wines. While Trace lay in his room sleeping, he lay there thinking of ways to woo her back into his life. He did still love her but the truth really was he needed her now. He needed her for so much but didn't want to lose her for anything. He wondered if he should just tell her the truth, thinking maybe this would be the best. But then she wouldn't believe he still loved her. He couldn't take that chance. He had to be very careful. Soon sleep overcame his worried mind and Jeronn slept a little more peaceful than he had in months. Even without a drink in his hand.

Chapter Eight

Trace woke up unaware of her surroundings. She turned over to face the sun. It felt good. As she opened her eyes and blinked a few times, she realized this wasn't her own room. She panicked. Had her worst fear come true? Was she in some deranged man's house that had recognized her and kidnapped her for money? She looked around the room. It was big and clean. There were two doors. Before she got out of the bed she checked between her legs to see if anything had happened to her. That was in check. She let her mind replay the events of last evening. "Oh my God Jeronn." she thought. She was actually in his home. She got up and opened the first door. It was a closet. A familiar scent came though. She was staring at a long line of silk suits and ties. All of different colors and styles. Shoes lined the extensive wall all neatly in place. She walked in the closet, which led to another door. She opened it. It was another entrance to the bathroom. The bathroom was huge. There was a long black marble counter with two sinks. The sinks both had gold faucets. No handles. It must have a sensor she thought. Mph. Nice touch. The Jacuzzi sized bathtub in the middle of the room was lovely. It had three long steps that led up to it. The towels matched everything. The shower on the other side of the room had no door. Just a shower that came out of the wall onto a tiled separated floor. Retha must've designed this for him she thought. She walked over to the mirrors and examined his cologne and after-shave. She picked them up to smell them. Trace what are you doing, she thought to herself. This is the last thing you need to be doing. Get yourself dressed and get the heck out of here. After staring at herself in the mirror for a long time, she decided that's exactly what she was going to do. *Lord,* she prayed as she washed her face, *I know that I've done so much wrong and yet everyday you bless me. For that I want to thank you for today. Dear Lord if this is where I'm supposed to be, I'll be. My only request is that if it is meant to be, Lord please make it go right. So I can change my ways. I don't want to sin any more. You know I don't. But I need your help. Amen."* She washed her face. In her mind as was everyday, she was washing away the sin from the day before. Washing away all the sin and hurt she felt to put on a new face. Trace wanted to start over and this was her chance. She looked up in the mirror and smiled. "Jeronn!" He startled her. He was standing directly behind her. He had the prettiest smile. It was like staring at the prettiest diamond in the whole jewelry store. She missed that smile so long ago. He was beautiful. He was her daybreak. She felt all these wonderful yearnings inside with him behind her. Standing there behind her reminded him of all those years ago when he would look at her body and take her whenever and wherever they were. It was morning and as always for a man, his whole body was awake. He didn't want to embarrass himself so he folded his hands in front of him and admired the view. She still had a wonderful body. All sugar and spice and smooth as chocolate. The way he remembered. He wished he could have her legs wrapped around his body right now. "Hello Beautiful." his voice cracked. She wanted to run and plant kisses all over his bashful little face. She knew why he was folding his hands, but she didn't want him to know she knew. He could always make her feel this way. It made him feel good that he could still make her smile. "Hi Jeronn." she finally spoke. "How long were you standing there?" She asked.

"Long enough to know you still have an ass like an eighteen year old." She gasped. She almost laughed. Not expecting an answer like that. She threw her towel at him. She walked to touch his face. "Thank you baby. Thank you for being in the right place at the right time. They stared into each other's eyes. Her feeling like he was her savior again and him wondering if she will ever forgive him for abandoning her all that time ago." "You are so beautiful." He spoke again. "You already said that." "I can't help it. You look so good in my shirt that I'm doing everything I can to keep my hands off you girl. So I think you should step back before my senses leave and I have my way with you." "Yeah right. You always

90

were a tiger in the morning. I guess you just can't keep that baby down huh?" She stopped short. "I'm sorry. I shouldn't have said that. Please forgive me. I guess I was just feeling a little too comfortable."

"Trace it's fine." He interjected. "You don't have to stop short with me. You know what I'm feeling. I know you feel it too." She did feel it. He made all her senses come alive. She felt warm under his shirt. She thought about letting nature take it's course thinking that would start things off right, but reality came into play and she hadn't forgotten how...Instead she turned away. This was her fresh start. She wasn't going to let sex or the past, ruin it for her. She wanted a chance to see how things could really be. She had sex with him the first night they met and now she was considering it again. Not this time she thought. Although she knew it would be the bomb. This time it's going to be done right or not at all she thought. "Let's eat."

Chapter Nine

Graham Watkins lay on the sidewalk with a pounding headache. He had images of the night before dancing around in his head. He couldn't think straight. He needed a cup of coffee. In the distance he made eye contact with a coffee shop. Giving his eyes time to adjust to the sun he did the best he could to dust off the dirt from his coat, wishing like hell he could go home and take a shower. "No. That bitch is there!" He said as if someone had asked him a question. He was not yet sober and his lips stuck together as he spoke. "I'll just wait till she goes to work and then go change my clothes." Again, he was explaining this to no one. Graham made his way across the street. He bought himself a newspaper and went inside the coffee shop.

The perky waitress who had watched him cross the street walked over to him and talked to him as if she were speaking to a two-year-old child. "Now, Sir, you know when you come in that door you have to have money don't you?" She said it with a silly little grin on her face. He frowned as if she were as dumb as she looked and decided to amuse himself. Hell he was almost feeling good for the start of his day. He spoke back to her in the same parent to child tone with a are-you-stupid grin on his face, "Now lady, you know if someone comes in that door you're supposed to be nice and take their orderrrr!" he sang. Immediately wiping the grin off his face.

Inside he was cracking up. The stupid look on the waitresses face gave

him satisfaction. "You know what? Black people aren't going anywhere

so you may as well just relax." He sat himself down at a clean table and

picked up a menu. "You know what? This ain't my station." She smiled

and strolled away.

As he scanned the menu a waitress bent over the table popping her gum in

his face. She stared at him while tapping her pad waiting for his order.

Graham couldn't concentrate on the menu for trying to stare at her big

breasts almost bursting through the green uniform she was wearing.

"What are you lookin' at?" she almost whispered. Although she full well

knew. She continued to pop her gum. She talked directly into his eyes.

"You like what you see baby?" Graham licked his lips trying to figure out

what type of game this red headed beauty was playing. He ignored her

and spoke "I'll just have a large coffee, black and a cheese danish. "Oh,"

she pretended to write. "Large black..." she let the words trail off. "Well

now, that sounds good. I'll be right back." He sat there trying to figure

out what she meant by 'large black' and 'that sounds good'. He was getting

hard in his pants. He took his coat off and sat there with his hands in his

lap. Not yet ready to read the paper, he just stared out the window,

completely forgetting about his plans to get back on his feet. The waitress returned with his coffee interrupting his thoughts. "Well now, after all the ruckus you made coming in the door I know you're not going sit there quietly now are you?" He turned to her. He just looked, waited. "Well so that's how it is?" she continued. "May I sit down?" she asked. She sat not waiting for an answer. It's my break and I would like to talk to you if I may." He sat there stirring his coffee looking into her big green eyes. Her full red lips engrossed him. "Listen mister." "Graham. My name is Graham." "That's an old man's name and you don't look like an old man, Graham." She was flirting now and he could tell. There was no questioning the look in her eyes. She was beautiful and as she sat there with her breasts on the table, he tried to figure out her angle. Not being able to ignore the growth between his legs. He had been with white women before, but they were all hookers. He had paid for the things they gave him. But this beautiful creature seemed as though she would serve it up to him for free just as quick as she had served his coffee. He only stared at her listening to the clink of his spoon as it touched the inside of his cup. "Listen, Graham, we are not prejudiced in here. 'Specially not me." She had a southern accent. The way she talked and stressed each syllable was making him warmer by the minute. "In fact, Graham, I like black people. My ex-boyfriend was a black man. I have nothin' against ya'. In fact, how 'bout I pay for that breakfast for ya?" "That's quite all right. I can handle it. Shouldn't you be getting back to work?" She had ruined his mood. He hadn't made those comments about black people in search of an answer from her. "As I said, Graham, I'm on my break and I wanted to spend it with you." She looked down at his hands. They were big and strong looking just the way she liked it. "Listen Graham," she hesitated not knowing how to approach him. She licked her lips "I think I'm gonna get off early an uh," she looked around and lowered her voice, "I was wondering' if you'd be so kind as to walk me home. I only live around the corner and uh, I don't like to go out in this little dress so early in the morning with all these folks staring at me. I'd feel a little uncomfortable." He considered this. This wasn't happening to him. A second ago he woke up on the sidewalk, drunk out of his mind. Finding a few dollars in his pocket, and now a beautiful waitress wanted him to walk her home. He reached for his coat. "Nuh-uh. Here take my key so you know I'm serious." She pulled it from her breast. "Now just go around back and meet me in the alley behind the diner, I'm gonna come out the back, I mean if that's okay with you Graham?" "That's fine. Take your time."

"When you leave I'll be right out back by time you get in the alley ok?"

"Sure. Don't keep me waiting."

"Sure nuff' Graham." She got up and walked away behind the counter. Graham was already imagining sliding those black stockings off her pretty, southern body. But since she wasn't a hooker, what could she possibly want with him? Graham had a thing for hookers, and he was fully aware of this desire. She must know I don't have any money. Hell she should be able to tell by how untidy he looked. *I'll just keep that in mind to myself* he mumbled. He was finally sobering up. The excitement of things to come made his adrenaline flow and the hangover was going away. He flicked his paper to the back to read the sports and came across the most exquisite looking black woman wearing a long beautiful gown on the second page. *It was her. The prostitute from yesterday.* He knew he had seen her before. She was famous. But she was a prostitute. How could that be? Boy was he shocked. This couldn't be right.

He couldn't believe it. The most beautiful black singer that had ever lived was in that prostitutes house and it was Trace Reese. Maybe I'm still drunk, he thought. Maybe that's not her. *But what if it is?* He asked himself. What if she was the beautiful woman in the paper? Maybe she was there for somebody else. Maybe she wasn't the hooker. What if she was the Madam? His fingers began to itch. They always itched like that when he felt he could get a lot of money from somewhere. His mind was racing and he was thinking fast. "How can I found out?" He said to the paper. "Who you talkin' to sugar?" The waitress was back with a pot of hot coffee in her hands. "Did you want more coffee Graham?"

"Uhh, No thank you. Uh I think I'm gonna be going now." "Oh okay," she whispered. "Well I'll just meet you around back in two minutes." *Oh crap*. He had already forgotten about her and the key. "Uh," He hesitated. "Now you're not gonna walk out on me are ya darlin'? I really need your...protection." She was an annoyance now. He had money on his mind.

"Ok see you in two minutes." As he was putting his coat on, she brushed past him letting her large breasts brush his arm. "Excuse me sir." she winked. He left the diner.

"Should I go, should I go?" He kept mumbling. Before he knew it, he was already in the alley. He left the newspaper tucked under one arm while she grabbed hold of the other. "So," she said, walking across the alley. "What do you have to find out?" "What do you mean?" "Well in the diner, when you were reading the paper you said, 'how can I found out?'" *Nosey heifer*! He thought. "I meant how can I find out your name without attracting attention to myself and before I knew it you were at my table." "Oh sweetie that's so cute, but all ya had to do was ask. My name is Sonya. Sonya Whittingham. Well here we are," she sang.

"I thought you lived around the corner. This is right across the alley. You could've walked back here. What do you really want?" Although, he already knew. "Well Graham, I think by now you should know." She flung her purse over her shoulder. "Graham, as I said my last boyfriend was a black man and um, well I haven't found anyone that could, shall I say, measure up, if you know what I mean?" And well Graham, please don't think that I do this type of thing everyday, 'cause I don't. It's just that, well you're a very strong looking, attractive man and I, well I became attracted to you the minute you told off that stupid Millie back there. The head waitress. I hate her. Well anyway," she was looking for a cigarette. "Anyway Graham," she blew out the smoke, "I just needed some company for a little while. That's all. I'm not after anything. I see you don't have much anyway." She smiled. "I saw you this morning where you were sleeping. I could tell right off that with a change of clothes and hot bath and shave you clean up sharply. I just wanna help you I guess. Anyway, Graham, don't make me stand out here explaining myself to you. You gonna put the key in the door or what? I'll make it worth your while. "Well now after a speech like that, how could I refuse?" "That's more like it."

After entering the apartment, he could see that she wasn't very well off herself. She had a few nice things. She had pictures of famous people she probably never met on her walls. "Let me guess, you're a waitress who came out here to be a star, didn't make it so you work hard for your money, right?" "Yeah, that about sums it up. I ran away a long time ago from home but that's a whole other story."

"I wanna talk about you Graham. I ran you some bath water. Why don't you go hop in and let me wash ya back and I know I have something you can put on later." "That's very nice of you Sonya. Sure. I'll be right out okay?" "Sure hon. And I'll be right in." After awhile Sonya came in the bathroom wearing nothing but a smile and Graham instantly drew his attention to the patch of red between her pale thighs. She giggled. "Oh" she giggled, "I'm a natural redhead. The carpet matches the drapes." She walked over to the tub and climbed in front of him. "Graham," her voice much deeper an sensual now, "I didn't know you were such a large man. You're very broad under that coat." "And you're very beautiful under that green uniform." he retorted. Graham had never spoken to a white woman this way before because usually the white women that ever let him touch them actually were hookers. But this woman was gentle...sweet in her own nature. Wearing her hair down the way she was, she looked almost surreal. Graham wasn't an ugly man. He was an attractive looking normal guy, but just a little down on his luck. He ran his own business for a while, but because of bad bets it went under. He'd been trying for a while to settle everyone he owed and take care of his wife, but being at home with her was unbearable. He rarely went home anymore. He always acknowledged to himself that although he was just less than six feet tall he could always hold his own. He could definitely play the role if he wanted to. He could be some good woman's dream come true, if some good woman would just let him. "Graham," she smiled, "I think I finally found somebody who measures up," she cooed. Her words made his penis grow larger and his ego sail higher. He was used to being rough and raunchy, but something about her made him want to make love. Made him want to reach down in his bag of tricks and lay it on her like no man has ever done before. He wasn't that old. *Hell I'm only thirty-nine. I can still roll with the best of 'em* he thought. While Graham sat there trying to decide what she wanted him to do, Sonya decided to show him. A minute later her head was bobbing up and down on him. Graham leaned his head back and looked up at the cracked paint in the ceiling. He closed his eyes to concentrate on how good her mouth felt. Her lips were warm and with every downward motion her breasts were rubbing his thighs. He looked down at her and touched her. But not rough like he would a hooker. Soft and gentle, like he would be doing to his wife if he still loved her. 'She's evil.' he thought. Shutting her out of his mind. He couldn't hold back anymore, he really had to have her now. He lifted her head up and they both stood up. Sonya looked up at him with doe eyes. The perkiness and hardness of her nipples told it all. He put his hands between her legs. The heat between her thighs told him all he needed or wanted to know. He got out of the tub and asked, "Where's your room?" She got out and led him to her room, which was just as small as her living room. He laid her on the bed with ease. He shoved the extra sheets and blankets to the floor. He noticed there was a picture of a little girl with red hair and two missing front teeth on her night table and turned it down. Not wanting to look at it and not wanting it to look at him. He stared at her. He was really beginning to like Sonya. He didn't want to her hurt her but this woman wanted him bad. He could tell. She wasn't complaining and nagging like his wife does when they're in the bedroom. She was comforting and obliging. She also wasn't waiting for payment from him. She really wanted him for him. She shoved herself back and spread her legs wider. Inviting him closer. Instead of just jumping in and ramming himself inside her, which is what his instincts would normally do, he decided to enjoy himself and take his time. Seeing as how she wanted it too. He lay beside her and spread her hair out around her. He put her soft hands on her breasts and told her to keep them there. He spread her legs wide. He kissed her gently on her forehead. He touched her gently. He caressed her firmly. Before he knew what took over him he began to bury his face in her waiting strawberry. Sonya squeezed her breasts so hard they left her handprints. But she didn't move them, because he told her not to. Graham enjoyed this. She went down on him as well and all he kept thinking to himself was, he didn't have to pay for it. Graham was in dreamland and if it was a dream he intended to take full advantage of it. He pleased her. He pleased her for almost an hour before they both couldn't wait anymore. By that time she was so wet from so many orgasms that he almost fell right in. They made love like two lovers who had known each other for two years instead of two hours. She clung to him. The size of his penis made her scream, but the depth of his passion made her give. She gave her whole self to him in that bed and Graham could tell. Graham, who had nothing, was getting something he had yearned for a long time and he was getting it for free. Respect. Just before it was over, he remembered the picture in the paper and thought about how rich he was going to be. The thought of that made his penis harder. He released with the force of ten men. Graham was having the best day he had had in a long time. He collapsed on top of her. They slept for hours.

Chapter Ten

Sitting across the table from Jeronn, she could tell how much he had really missed her. All he could think of now was Trace. Despite the fact that he needed her, he was still enchanted by her. She was everything Retha was not. Trace was real. Even after all these years. She was real. He never told her but nights after they would make love he would just stare at her in the moonlight. He loved the beautiful shimmer of her soft ebony skin. He loved every curve of her voluptuous body. He remembered the way her breath would catch and she would arch her back whenever he touched her. He remembered how hard it was to let her go. He remembered how bad he felt when he thought he had to. "I've been such a fool Trace." he began. She didn't say anything. She continued eating. "Trace did you hear me? I said I was a fool." She chewed slowly. "I heard you Jeronn, but please don't."

"Please let me! I want to be here for you now. I've changed. I was hoping we could work something out." He spoke quickly. "Maybe we could be a family again. I don't know." She dropped her fork. "Jeronn, do you know how long I've waited to hear you say that to me? That you have made a mistake and you want me back? And now that you have, I guess I just don't feel any satisfaction. Jeronn I want to look at this as my rebirth.

I want to start over and forget the past. Seeing you yesterday, made me realize how far off the road I have taken my life. And now I need to redo this thing again. Yesterday before I fell asleep, I remember feeling that I do still love you. I could go on and not trust but it'd be a waste of my time." She lowered her voice and got up from her seat. "It'll be a waste of time because baby I know you love me too. I can see it in your eyes Jeronn. But there is something going on that you're not telling me so instead of getting into all that right now, lets just let it go for now and move ahead okay?" She smiled. "You know you're still the finest black woman God ever made don't you?" "And you're still talking the sweetest talk." He was too close. She stepped back. He pulled her closer. "Trace," He whispered heavily in her ear. "Let me love you. Let me love you now." She put her arms around him, "Jeronn, Baby, I want that too. But can you forget where you found me and still love me unconditionally?" He looked in her eyes and kissed her. Kissed her long and hard on the mouth. She was breathless. Her lips tasted so good. He tasted so real. It was Jeronn in a way she couldn't remember, but he was all there nonetheless. "Jeronn, I can't. Even though you didn't answer my question, I don't think I can even love myself unconditionally after the way you found me. So please don't." Her stomach was turning. Aching for the true affection she knew he could give.

He kissed her gently on the neck. She could feel herself giving in. He was on the verge of stripping when reality hit him. He wasn't thinking with his head. He was thinking with his body and right then he didn't think he could forget. "Maybe you're right. I think we should wait. He put her at arms length away. He realized that she needed time to heal inside emotionally and time to just rest from work. He knew he had a lot do with what she'd been doing. That just doesn't sit right with him.

"So many times after you put me out I felt like a punk living with Retha. Now that I see you I feel even worse. I just want everything to be absolutely right this time. Trust me Trace, it can happen, if we take our time. You've been a single mother and a career woman and a part time pro..." He let his sentence trail wishing he could swallow those last words as quickly as he'd said them.

"A what Jeronn? You can say it. A mother, a career woman and a part time whore!" she ordered. "Maybe you're right. Maybe I do need professional help. And I'll get it. But you know, I was wrong about thinking I could fly off into some damned lala land with you and act like nothing happened. There I go being ignorant again. Well thanks for the reality check Jeronn Montarius Clark. I owe you one. And now I'm leaving." "Trace, don't do this. I didn't mean to say it, but hell what am I supposed to say? What am I supposed to call what you've been doing?"

She was up the stairs and already gone. He thought he should go after her and get her. But his heart told him this was not the right way. She wanted to start over the right way and he would help her no matter what it took. He waited for her downstairs to take her home.

It's not his fault he found her in that apartment. "Jeronn, I'm sorry." She apologized as she returned down the stairs. I know you're only trying to help. I guess I'm just a little sensitive when it comes to you and the things you say. I don't want you to have to tread lightly on every word you say to me. I guess you need some one to talk to as well. I don't know what you've been going through, but coming to see a hooker must mean there's something drastically wrong. And finding me there must have cut you a pretty hard blow so I want to apologize and tell you that you are not to blame for the wrongs I've done and I apologize if I made you feel that way." She walked closer to him. "Forgive me." He said. "I was wrong again. I want to help. I took a wrong step but I've backed up now and I was wrong. Right now let's get you home and take care of business step by step."

"Cool let me call Chanelle first. She's probably worried and angry with me for not calling. Plus she'll be happy to see you."

"I actually spoke to Chanelle last night. She already knows I'm coming and she's fine with it. "Boy, still taking care of everything aren't you?"

"I'm trying." On the way to Trace's house neither spoke. Jeronn still couldn't figure out how to begin the subject of needing her help. Trace was remembering how they had written lots of songs together. These were songs she was sure that he would have Retha recording, but she never heard them on the radio so she guess he just aborted the ideas.

When Graham woke up he felt like he had been sleeping for two days. He hadn't had such a peaceful sleep in such a long time. He called out to Sonya but there was no answer. He got up to go to the bathroom and wash his face and he found a note on the mirror. It said she'd be back in a couple of hours. Graham had no intention of sticking around for that. Besides he didn't know how long she had been gone already so he decided on a hasty exit. He put on his clothes, grabbed a beer from the refrigerator and headed home. When he got there he was hoping his wife wouldn't be around and she wasn't. He was still feeling pretty good about the information he found in the newspaper earlier that day and hoped that maybe he would be rich soon enough. He turned on the stereo and headed for the shower. His plan was to return to the apartment and hopefully find the singer there again. If she was who he thought she was, he knew she would be there. He also didn't want to be arrested in case he was wrong. But for some reason he didn't feel he was. He was standing in the mirror shaving and singing his favorite song when he heard the front door open and close. He knew there would be some grief about not coming home last night. He was putting on his aftershave when the bathroom door opened. "Close the door Lonnie you'll let the steam out." "Fine." she said and walked in and closed the door behind her.

"Can't you wait until I come out?" he hissed. "Nope." She folded her arms. "Why you lookin' at me like that?" he asked.

"No reason." She was unusually quiet to him. He expected her to be barking the minute she saw him, but she didn't. "So who's the slut got you wanting to put aftershave on yo' dirty ass face?" "Don't start. Pleeease?" he begged. "Ain't no woman got to make me do nothing and can't make me do nothing. You should know that by now."

"You know what Gray. You're right. I'm not even about to start with you today. But you know what? I'm your wife and this has been going on too long. Now are we going to work this thing out or are you going to move on? You can't keep coming up in here anytime you feel like it and doing whatever the hell you wanna do and don't take care of your home. I mean how you just gone come in here and drink up all the beer and use my razor and do whatever the heck you want to up in here? And you don't even pay any bills no more." "Lonnie, do we have to do this right now? Didn't you just say you weren't going to start this with me? Man! And first of all I only drank one funky beer."

"Well, I only had two."

"AAANNdd...Excuse me, I bought these razors for you anyway. Not only that, I am on the verge of something big that you wouldn't even be able to handle so believe me sweetie, first chance I get I'm outta your hair."

"I'm sick of you and these get rich quick schemes Gray. Now what's this one all about?" "None'o yo' damn business and if you don't mind I need a little privacy." Lonnie rolled her eyes at him just before she walked out and closed the door. She swung it back open to ask him a question and accidentally bumped his arm. "Ooowww!! What the hell!"

"Ooooh Graham I'm sorry. Let me see. I didn't mean to do that." He held his chin up for her to look. She smacked her lips.

"Oh hell that ain't nothing. I wanted to ask you what do you want for dinner?"

"You came in here to ask me that? Get the hell outta here and close the door."

"Forget you Graham. Before you leave we are going to talk." After he shaved he went into the bedroom to decide what he would be wearing for the night. She had at least done his laundry for him. That was cool. He stood in the doorway of the closet trying to decide what tonight would bring him. He could smell her cooking dinner downstairs and decided to lie on the bed and watch some television before getting dressed. His

stomach was growling and if he didn't bother her maybe he could get

through dinner without a bunch of conversation. He put on his satin

boxers and black socks. He grabbed his robe. He was clicking the

channels and settled on Sally Jesse. The show was about women getting

makeovers. He watched for a while and decided that some of these

women didn't look half bad once they combed their hair and put on a nice

outfit. One thing he could say about his wife, she dressed modestly but

with her clothes off she was a fox. Smooth brown skin and thick legs.

Just what he liked. He could hear her marching up the stairs now and he

prepared for war. She came in the bedroom and his back was to her. She

thought he was sleeping so she walked over and turned off the television.

"What did you do that for?" he asked.

"You know you were sleep don't even try it."

"I wasn't sleeping now could you turn it back on please?" She clicked the

television back on and he turned the channel away from Sally with the

remote. She sat on the bed at his feet and stared at him. He looked good.

He always looked good. She loved the hair on his chest. She wanted to

play in it. He didn't dare turn around to look at her. This might start a

conversation he thought. He buried his head deeper in the pillow to let her

know he didn't want to be bothered. She began to undress. He was her husband after all. She could give him a little somethin' somethin.' Mostly

to satisfy herself. I mean he hadn't been around a lot and she did have

needs. She slipped into the bed next to him and began rubbing his back.

He didn't know she was undressed because he still had on his robe.

"Want a massage?"

"Nope! Cause all you gone do is get me relaxed and start fussing at me

again. I'm not in the mood."

"I promise no fussing." She pulled his robe from his shoulders and began

to massage him. She straddled his back and rubbed deep rings into the

small of his back. She told him to turn over. He did. He saw she was

naked and immediately became aroused. Her bare breasts were beautiful.

He smiled at her. She smiled at him. Deep down they still loved each

other. There had been so much going on between them that one thing

always led to another. They made love quietly and lovingly. There was

nothing to be said. They just held each other and watched TV. They

made their way downstairs and had dinner together. They occasionally

glanced at one another and smiled. Graham had not felt this warm towards

his wife in a long time. He appreciated the silence. He knew she was

probably right about him always coming up with some idea about how to

get rich. He didn't know why he had this way of thinking. What he did

know, is that he didn't want to work for anybody. He had had a nice job and he lost it. That was almost a year ago. His wife had been supportive in the beginning but then she began to nag him all the time about needing help around the house. Then she began nagging him about helping to pay the bills. The truth is he really did want to help out, he just couldn't bring himself to work for someone else anymore. He just wanted her support a little while he tried to figure it out. He knew that his little time just grew and grew but he didn't want to be reminded all the time. Tonight there was none of that. He appreciated it. He knew she probably wanted to let him have it, but in the spirit of the time they just shared together he realized they both would just ignore it for now. He thought that if this thing with the singer panned out he would definitely try to work things out with his wife. He couldn't wait to see the smile on her face when she saw how much cash he would have. He would be set for a long time until he decided what he would do with himself. At least that's the plan. After dinner they sat on the sofa drinking coffee and reading the newspaper. This was something they both hadn't done in a long time. They simply sat together and enjoyed each other's company. "Would you like a glass of wine?" Lonnie asked. "Sure." "I was saving this for a special occasion, but I guess this is as nice as any." She smiled. She gave him a glass. She clinked her glass to his and they smiled. Graham hadn't been this relaxed in a long time. He momentarily thought about Sonya. He pushed her to the back of his mind. He had thought about sharing his wealth with her since she was so nice to him, but Lonnie was his wife. He wanted to do something nice for her even if they didn't stay together. After their drinks they made their way upstairs to watch TV in their bedroom. They cuddled and fell asleep watching TV. Graham woke up in the middle of the night to go to the bathroom. When he returned Lonnie was buried under the covers snoring softly. The day hadn't turned out at all like he expected. He woke up on the street not knowing when he passed out. He slept with a beautiful redhead who he was thinking of potentially spending some time with. But his wife? Today of all days she was the sweetest thing in the world. He hadn't been with her so intimately in such a long time. He was filled with love for her right now. She had been so patient with so many things he had done wrong. She had a right to complain. He knew it. He just didn't want to face his doubts like a man. But that would all change once he came into his money. Graham lay on the bed next to Lonnie. She smelled so nice. He turned his body closer to her and slept peacefully with his wife. Lonnie Watkins. He loved her.

Chapter Eleven

The next couple of weeks went by as Graham randomly staked out the apartment he had seen Trace coming out of. He hadn't seen her there in all that time so he assumed he might have had the wrong place after all. Besides he wouldn't have expected to find a prostitute in that neighborhood anyway. He had heard about this wonderful lady of the evening while standing outside of a French restaurant hailing a cab. He heard a gentleman say that he was going to see 'his regular' he called her. They discussed it at small length. Enough for him to know it was a prostitute and get the address because the guy was hailing a cab too. When he had gone to see the woman a few weeks earlier he had won the lottery and had plenty of money on him. He was willing to pay the price of a high priced hooker if it had guys like the one he had seen coming back for more. But after not being able to get to the woman he thought he was coming to see he just spent the evening drinking. He didn't want to go home at the time so he drank himself senseless until he passed out and woke up and discovered all his money he was gone. He and Lonnie had been getting along pretty good for the past few weeks and he didn't want that to end. He even stood outside of the restaurant where he met Sonya and thought about going in but passed on by when he thought about

Lonnie. He really did love her. He remembered when they got married. She was so beautiful. He had never felt that way about any other woman in his life. When she discovered she couldn't have children, their lives changed a lot. She was easily upset and less tolerant of anything he did. When he lost his job that was the end all. She absolutely didn't take anything from him. He hated being around her. They were always at each other's throats. Many times he would try to tell her that it didn't matter that they couldn't have children, but he knew that more than anything that's what she wanted. She wanted her man and she wanted some babies. That's what she always told him. He really missed how cool they used to be. He figured once he came into his money they would be that way again. He would take her away on an exotic trip and make love to her for days. He wanted to give back to her all the time and love she had given to him. But it couldn't happen if this famous prostitute never showed up. He was getting tired of staking out a place where no one showed up.

Jeronn and Trace spent the next few weeks getting to know each other again. He escorted her to some of her studio sessions and some photo shoots and he really saw how well she really was doing. Better than he could ever imagine. He knew it wouldn't be long before the tongues would start wagging and the world would wonder if they were a couple again. He had already seen a small article in a gossip magazine. It was disguised as one of those 'guess who's dating whom' columns but he figured they were talking about them. He didn't mention it to her. He didn't want there to be any more pressure added to what could be the rest of their lives. There were times he wanted to mention to her how much he really needed her help. But how could he tell her all about it without upsetting the nature of their relationship. They were driving back from a wonderful picnic at the beach. It was a nice long peaceful drive. He popped in an old cd. She smiled. It was an old song they had written together. It seemed different by it being so long ago. Back then everything was smooth and romantic. Now everything was hip-hop and more than rhythm than blues.

"I thought I'd hear Retha singing that song by now. Why didn't you let her do it?"

"Retha didn't have what you have. It took me a long time to realize that. For a long time we searched for a song for her to do but nothing ever came of it. Nothing was ever right. In my eyes she had the look but little talent. In her eyes she had the look and the talent but stupid me who wasn't projecting her image good enough. Boy she was a nut case. I'm sorry." He laughed. "I didn't mean to say all those things about that nut ball. Besides I know some of the things I say, hurt you." She tucked in her lips and smiled. "Are you trying to get on my good side Jeronn?"

"I thought I was already on your good side?" he asked.

"Anyway."

"Yeah. Anyway. " He cleared his throat.

"Trace what would you say to us uh,"

"Starting over?" She finished his sentence.

"Well yeah, but not only that." He licked his lips.

"I mean, um Trace here it is. Retha and I got a divorce recently."

"When?"

He sighed. "It was months ago and um," He gripped the steering wheel.

"Well um, maybe we ought to talk about this when you have less on your

mind." "No Jeronn. Stop doing that. I'm cool. Let's talk about it now. I

had a wonderful day with you and I feel I can handle this conversation

right now. So what's up?"

"Trace. Not now. I'm not completely over it." he lied. He just didn't have

the nerve to ask her for the financial help he needed. Or to tell her about

the trouble he was in with his little problem. It wasn't the time. He wasn't

ready to tell her the truth about Retha taking everything from him. Most

of his money and royalties and all were either tied up or no longer an

option. He didn't want to tell her that he had gotten caught up in drugs and

drinking so much that he didn't know his head from his tail. Trace meant a lot to him so telling her right now would only make her think he was trying to use her and that was the last thing from his mind. He had to make sure all of his real reasons were in check. Besides, he owed a lot of people as well. Big people in high places. People who had supported his and Retha's outlandish promotions and ideas to make her a big star. She turned out to only be a big problem. In the beginning it all worked fine. But she never could live up to Trace. She was always accusing him of still loving Trace and wanting to be with Trace because her career was better. She accused him many late nights of being out with Trace. No matter how true she was about his feelings for Trace he never told her so. He had never even seen Trace that close up until weeks ago. Trace was a sensible woman who could have it all without trying. Trace was also the only person he knew who would ever help him. As rich as she had become, he thought she would never be in his presence again. Not after the way he treated her all those years ago. They hardly bumped into each other over the years and she had become a much bigger star than he had ever anticipated. She was at every award show. Some place or another was always having her as a special guest star. Big or small event she was there. She knew what she was doing. And he could have been right there with her had he not abandoned her. The truth was he really didn't deserve her help. If being by her side while she recovered was what she needed, he was going to be there.

"So whatever happened to all your old friends?" She interrupted his thoughts.

"What friends? The dudes I grew up with?"

"Yeah?"

"I talked to those guys a few months ago. They're all doing the same thing. They're working and doing things in the community. Nothings changed."

"You've changed?"

"How so?" he asked. She wanted him to spill his guts but he wasn't going for it. She could wait. "We're here?" Every time they had pulled up to her home these past few weeks she became nervous. She thought about being alone with him sometimes. Every time she came home Maja was there and it made it easier. Maja was glad to see Jeronn the day she brought him over. They laughed and talked like nothing had changed. But of course it had. Chanelle had her own daughter with a baby's daddy away at college. At least he wasn't a drug dealer or something, not willing to take care of them. She was thankful he was doing something with his life. She knew Chanelle would love to finish her education. When she was ready, she'd go back and she would support her. They held hands walking through the door. Maja came in holding the baby. "Hello precious."

Maja immediately began the rundown of the day and where Chanelle was and all her messages from her agent and such. They discussed the plan for dinner, which was, she really didn't have a plan. Not tonight anyway. She didn't know what she would have to do and she would check her calendar. Maja told her that her agent was on his way over to talk and should be here shortly. She set up a bar in the library for her guest. Trace was busy entertaining Jeronn when Ross Langley walked in. "Trace baby where have you been? I've been calling all over for you." "Well, I turned off my cell phone Ross. I wanted to spend a quiet day with Jeronn." Ross glanced over at Jeronn. Barely acknowledging him. He knew Trace and Jeronn's history and he didn't think it was a good idea at all that she be seeing him again. He made an effort to do some checking on Jeronn and first chance he got he was going to tell Trace all about him. Ross poured himself a drink and sat down at her desk, as he had done many times before. He wanted Jeronn to see he had free reign of the place and he was marking his territory. He would love to have had Trace as his own. She would never warm up to him. He didn't understand why. After all he was a good-looking guy. Well dressed and he had plenty of money, but she never held any torch for him. Hell, she didn't even hold a match flame for him. He knew a long time ago it was because of the way Jeronn had treated her, but he thought if he were just patient with her she would come around. Sometimes he could never find her though. He put a detective on her once, but discovered that she just had another little apartment. Nothing for him to be alarmed about. He figured it was her sanctuary and left it alone. He desperately wanted to be a part of her life, but she would never give him a chance. And now, Jeronn. Jeronn seemed to be dripping his way back on the scene little by little and he didn't like it one bit. He opened a drawer and pulled out a cigar. Clipped the end, lit it and blew smoke in the air to let Jeronn know he knew where everything was and to give him the impression that he was quite familiar with everything there was to know about Trace. "So RL what's been up?" She walked over and sat on the edge of the desk. "Well, we still have to discuss if you want to tour this year or if you want to just go in the studio. Right now baby doll it's your show and you can pretty much do what you like. As far as any meetings go I'll have my secretary fax over your agenda. The one thing I can say up front is the Oprah Winfrey show is running it's last season and she wants you to be on the show before she's all booked up. You need to confirm baby doll." "Well,"

"Great. I'll take care of it." "RL I haven't agreed to anything yet."

"Trust me Trace baby. I know you. When you hesitate like that I already know you'll say yes." He glanced at Jeronn after making that comment. Jeronn was keeping himself busy checking out her library. Trying to pretend he wasn't listening. He didn't like Ross Langley the minute he stepped into the room. With his fancy tailor made suit and alligator shoes. His Movado watch and his perfect goatee. Who did he think he was anyway? Making himself at home like that. Trying to flex like he and Trace had something going on. He knew the routine. What he didn't know is, if something actually had gone on between he and Trace. Trace wasn't stopping him from doing his little rooster dance all over her library. Look at her over there smiling and carrying on. Giving him all teeth. If she smiled anymore the corner of her lips would meet at the back of her neck. Ross was checking out his envy. He could see it all over his face. He didn't care. Trace was just where he wanted her. Trace could also see that Jeronn was a little annoyed. He sighed one too many times before she realized the situation. Secretly she enjoyed this opportunity to make him jealous but she couldn't follow through. Trace knew Jeronn knew what she was up to in her life. She couldn't pretend with Jeronn the way she could with Ross. She knew Ross was sweet on her. But he was just too slick for her. He was fine though. Many nights she wanted to get with the brother. She didn't want to open herself up to any type of relationship though. Ross told her he could confirm her doing the show with Oprah and that she needed to come to his office sometime later in the week, he needed to inform her of some things. He said it a little loudly to make sure that Jeronn heard him, but she didn't know why. Jeronn knew. He was afraid that Ross had been doing some snooping around his affairs. He knew he had better come clean with Trace before Ross could. Maja came in to ask Ross if he would be staying for dinner. Ross told her no, he had plans for the night but that he would love to come over later in the week if she would make his favorite again. With that bit of information left in the air he made his exit. Not before telling Jeronn how good it was to see him out and about. Like he was some sort of washed up producer. Jeronn acted the perfect gentleman and told him he was sorry he wasn't staying to share dinner with them. That he and Trace would love to have him over sometime soon. Trace enjoyed the game they were playing. They were just flexing. She wouldn't get in the middle of it. She had enough to think about. After dinner Jeronn stayed a little longer for coffee and to play with the baby. Chanelle told him more about her boyfriend and how she knew he would be proposing soon. She wasn't worried and told Jeronn that he shouldn't worry either. There will be no shotgun wedding. After having coffee Chanelle told them goodnight, she was going to put the baby to bed before some of her friends came over for awhile. She told her mom, they would be in the pool house so they wouldn't disturb her or the baby. "Jeronn are you staying over tonight?" They both looked up at her wondering where that came from. Jeronn smiled and told her "no but nice try." She grabbed some grapes and left. "Are you sure you won't stay Jeronn? We have a few guest rooms if you'd like to have a nightcap. Maybe listen to some music?" How could he say no to that? They went back into the library, turned on the stereo, lit a nice low fire and chilled. They sat on the leather sofa and chit chatted. Jeronn finally came around to asking her what was up with Ross Langley. She laughed. "Don't worry about RL. He's been trying to woo me since he came on the scene. I just don't find him attractive is all. I mean, yes he's good looking, the man can hang a suit and he's..." she stopped herself.

"Oh, I'm sorry. I shouldn't be talkin' about that brotha." "Don't stop on my account." He teased as he sipped his brandy. "Well I shouldn't be telling you all this."

"No it's cool. I'm a big boy. Knock yaself out."

"Oh yeah? Well what was up with that verbal wrestling you two were doing in here earlier?" "Aw, baby. That's just something guys do. Don't even trip about that. But I would like to know if you ever had anything at all going on with him? I mean brotha man was all over the place like he knew you intimately." "Well. He does know a lot about me. I pay him to know a lot about me. I can't afford him to screw up one little thing. Aside from the way you saw him today. I run a tight ship. When it comes to my career, hey, ain't no half steppin." "Well, I'm glad to hear that. So what do you think he wants to fill you in on later this week besides the Oprah show?" He asked casually. He didn't know when the right time would be to tell her all what's up with him. "I don't know. Could be anything. You never know with Ross. He's been out of his mind trying to find out what I'm always doing with my time. I think he knows I have an apartment. He just doesn't know what I've been doing." "Trace I have to ask. How come no one has discovered who you are? I mean, aren't you afraid of exposure." "You know what? I used to be. Not anymore. I find myself in the company of men who only have one thing on their minds. They're rich, they're lonely and they're depressed about something. They're so wrapped up in their own world, they're not thinking about me. It's not even about me. These are guys who don't sit around watching TV and reading magazines all day. You know what I mean? Most times it's late at night and I go there to be alone and well you know. Sometimes I disguise myself. Wear different make up. Different hairstyle. Different wig. Different persona. I know, it sounds crazy right?"

"What you got some kind of split personality or something?" "Ha. If only. But the truth is a person with a split personality would have no idea what the other personality is doing with out intense therapy. No, I know what I'm doing. Well, I did. Lots of times I go there because I get so lonely. Just want some company. I don't get as many visitors as you may think.

But sometimes I do. I guess because I'm not there regularly." "How have men heard about you?" She cleared her throat. "Well, let's see..." She was swirling her drink. "One night, I was at a premier party and I won't name any names but I connected with someone. One thing led to another and before I knew it we were back at my apartment. It wasn't until morning that I realized this genius doesn't even know who I am. With that in mind, I made his butt pay for my time and told him if he breathed a word to anyone where I lived, I would expose him for the lame brain that he was. Well, he forked over lots of dough and became a regular. Just knocking on my door anytime he felt like it. Sometimes just to talk. Well, he still had no idea who I was and he asked me if he could refer one of his friends to come and talk to me and I said sure. Well, so that he wouldn't recognize who I was, I bought a wig, some cheap perfume and changed my voice and there it was. Immediate actress! Well, I soon discovered that the men I was dealing with were real geeks. That's why they had no idea who I was. They were into making lots of money and not much more. I could never date any of them. Although there were times when I was quite attracted to a few guys. But, it never happened. Anyway, I stopped going to my apartment for a while so that people would get the message not to come back. It pretty much worked. I got the occasional visit. And then boom. There you were. My knight in shining armor. Which by the way, you still haven't told me why you were there. Certainly you weren't there just because you were divorced and couldn't find a woman." "Well," now he cleared his throat. He was wondering if this was the right time to tell her everything. To tell her the situation he found himself in. "Well?" she pushed. "Well, uh...it's complicated." he sighed. "I was feeling a little low myself. I had actually obtained the address at a fundraiser. I overheard one of the big wigs telling another big wig that if he were ever in a situation to go to this address. Well, the truth is I had no idea what to expect. But the other guy laid the matchbook down and I picked it up. I wanted to find out myself what this was all about."

"Oh really? And what kind of situation are you in?" "Well, the situation I'm in, is not the situation I expected when I opened the door." "What type of situation is it?"

"Well, I'm still not quite ready to talk about it." He chickened out. "I'm actually getting tired. I better get going." "Oh. Well, if that's what you want to do." "Yeah. I better get going. I will give you a call tomorrow if that's okay."

"Of course." She walked him to the door. She didn't want him to leave, but if he thought it was best she would let him go. Her heart ached to watch him go. She was afraid she was falling deeply in love with him all over again. But he has his secrets she thought. She wondered if that would ever change.

Chapter Twelve

Jeronn drove towards home thinking about the whole day with Trace. He was definitely going to have to tell her what's going on with him before *Ross Langley* could. What kind of man was he anyway? She just went on and on about how good he looked and how much money he had. How would she feel if Ross Langley disappeared from the face of the earth? He wondered what Ross wanted to tell her anyway. Maybe it was his imagination. How could he found out anything about him anyway? He was always careful to keep his secret just that, a secret. He would just have to pay him a little visit tomorrow. On his way home Jeronn stopped to buy himself something to drink. He was going to need a little help getting to sleep tonight.

Graham hadn't gotten anywhere with his hunt for the mysterious woman. He had staked out her apartment for weeks and was unable to find her. No one had come or gone since the first time he was there. He was beginning to think what the woman told him was true. The woman he was looking for no longer lived there and he actually did have the wrong woman. Today he was tired of waiting outside and he was afraid people were beginning to wonder who this man was hanging around in the area. When nightfall came he decided to break his way into the apartment. He slipped in unnoticed. The moon lit up the room enough to find a lamp. He turned it on quietly and searched the room. It smelled wonderful. It smelled like leather and perfume. He could tell no one had been there in awhile. Dust was beginning to form on the cocktail table. There were two glasses on the table but they had been there for a while. There was a dead bug floating in one of them. He made his way into the kitchen. There wasn't much there. Mostly wine and cheese and brandy. Entertainment food, he thought. He looked in the refrigerator and took out a beer. There were no pictures on the wall to tell him where he was. He made his way into the bedroom. The bed was made and there was a nightgown across it. It was pretty. He picked it up to examine it better. It smelled nice. He laid it back on the bed just the way he found it. He went to the stand by the bed and looked in the drawer. There was a pack of cigarettes and two boxes of condoms. "Magnums, hmph." One box was opened and one wasn't he noticed. Nothing here to indicate this woman was a prostitute. He went and looked in the closet. There were a few suits, nice ones. Nice shoes. Nice jewelry. Nothing fancy. There were two bottles on the chest of drawers. There was a very expensive bottle of perfume and a cheap one. The cheap one was barely used. He looked in the drawers. The top drawer had a sandwich bag half full of marijuana and top papers. The drawers weren't that full either. The bedroom and the refrigerator looked as if no one ever lived there. Again he thought, maybe the woman he was looking for did actually move. Maybe he actually did have the wrong person. He was beginning to feel bad. He had been promising Lonnie that he would have something nice for her soon. Now it looked like his plan wouldn't work. He was actually breaking the law and trespassing into someone's personal life. He was all for making a quick buck, but he would never go this far into breaking the law. Now what was he going to do? He was headed towards the living room when he noticed something at the door. He hadn't noticed it when he walked in. There were several little slips of paper under the door. He slowly walked over to retrieve them in case the deliverer was still standing outside the door. He didn't want to be heard. He slowly crept over and peeped out the hole. No one was there. He picked up the papers. *Miss Lady. I miss you. Please come back to me.* That was one. *Babydoll, where have you been? I desperately need your love.* These could be from her lover he thought. There was nothing to indicate anything suspicious. The last note was his moneymaker he thought. *Honey, you cant make any money if you don't answer the door. Hope to see you soon. Den.* That was his only clue that this could still be the place. If the prostitute had moved out then when Trace comes she'll be shocked at these notes. But if she hadn't moved out then Miss Trace Reese was the whore he thought she was. He felt this warranted a few more trips in this neighborhood to try and catch her. In the meantime, he had better get out of this apartment in case he was seen. He went to the refrigerator and took a whole six-pack. He grabbed a few condoms from the bedroom stand. He turned out all the lights and headed for the door. He put the notes back on the floor where he had found them. He gently closed the door behind him and left. Lonnie had let him drive her car so he had better hurry home before she gets pissed off about him being gone so long. But first he wanted to stop by the restaurant and see Sonya. He felt like getting a little freaky tonight. It wouldn't take long. And he knew she'd be more than willing. He drove to the restaurant where she worked but he didn't see her inside. He drove around the block and went to her apartment. He heard the radio on, but didn't hear anyone inside. He felt stupid standing there holding a six-pack with condoms in his pocket. What if she already had company? He would look like a total fool. *Nope. I ain't going out like that* he thought. He turned to walk away. Then he heard her laugh. He went back up the steps and listened closely at the door. He didn't hear anything else, just her laughing. He softly knocked on the door, bracing himself for some big dude to come to the door. After all, she did say she liked brothers. He heard her come to the door and peek through the hole. There was a pause. He could tell she was hesitating. He turned his head as if he were looking downstairs so she could see him fully. She opened the door with a big grin on her face.

"Well, shuga. I didn't think I'd be seein' Y'all again." "May I come in?"

"Of course," she moved back for him to enter. He noticed she had decorated a little bit. The apartment smelled real nice like peaches. She had some candles lit and she was obviously reading the newspaper. She had it sprawled on the couch.

"So what did I hear you laughing at when I was coming up the stairs?"

"Oh." she replied. "I love Garfield. That is one crazy cat." She began to laugh almost hysterically.

"May I sit down?"

"Oh sure." She moved the paper from the couch. He put the six-pack on the floor next to his feet. He crossed his legs and looked around.

"Something bothering you?"

"Oh no. I was just taking a look around. The last time I was here I was still a little intoxicated." "And a bit distracted I might add." He smiled.

"So what brings you over?"

"I was in the neighborhood and thought I'd stop by." "Really? What were you doin' in the neighborhood?" "Oh, just checking some things out. What have you been up to?" "Nothing. Just working and looking for something better." He really didn't feel like chitchatting. He wanted to

get down to business so he could go home to Lonnie. She bent down and

opened one of the beers and drank most of it down. She sat a little bit

closer to him. Sensing what he wanted. He didn't want to kiss her. He

just wanted the business. Since Lonnie wasn't getting on his nerves

lately, he did feel a little bit guilty. But hey, she came on to him and

obviously there were no strings attached. She took a sip of her beer and

got on her knees. She started unbuckling his belt. He tried not to look at

her directly. He focused on the red nail polish on her toes instead. But

that didn't really turn him on so he focused on her breasts, which were

looking huge since she was leaning over him. *What the hell?* He'd get

what he wanted and be on his merry way. She stopped what she was

doing and went to the bedroom. She returned naked with a condom

between her teeth. He didn't want to have sex with her he thought. *Now I

gotta take all my clothes off, have sex with this woman, take a shower so

Lonnie won't be able to tell and...Man!!* He really didn't want to do this

now. Cheating on Lonnie tonight looked like too much trouble when he

could just go home to her and get everything he wanted and some dinner

afterwards. *Hmph! Well, I gotta finish what I started. I'll just make it

quick. He* thought. He actually didn't have to take his clothes off. After

she put the condom on him she assumed a doggie style position. He just let his pants fall to his ankles and got behind her. She was moaning and groaning so much that he couldn't help but get it over quickly. It wasn't exactly what he wanted but it was good. He grabbed his pants up and penguin walked to the bathroom. He removed the condom and took a towel from the hamper. He didn't feel like looking around for a clean one or asking for one. He cleaned himself as best he could with hot water and soap. He stood looking in the mirror trying to decide how to get out of here quickly. He made his way back into the living area and sat down. She put on her robe and was reading the paper and drinking a beer when he returned. "So uh." He started. She smiled. "Hey baby. You don't have to say anything. No strings attached." He felt relieved and a little awkward since she said it out loud but what could he do? He was married and there couldn't possibly be anything serious between them. When he first met her he thought he might want to share the wealth with her but he now realized it was the hangover talking. He and this beautiful redheaded creature could never have anything together. Not as long as he was married. And he didn't want to leave Lonnie. "Well, I guess I better get going. But if you ever need anything."

"I'll be fine Graham. I do thank you for stopping by. Lets me know you were at least thinking about me. "

"Oh by the way," he pulled some cash from his pocket "Oh Graham you don't have to do that. You don't have to do that at all. I'll be fine."

"I'm sure you will." "Can I have one of your beers before you go?" "You can have them all. Well, I guess I'll be going." "Bye Graham." He felt guilty when he closed the door behind him. It was too easy. She had the most beautiful smile. He hadn't noticed it before, but she was absolutely gorgeous. Well, no use thinking about what you can't have. He made his way home to Lonnie who had candles lit all over the house and romantic music. The house smelled nice. Lonnie always kept the house clean. He could hear her upstairs in the bedroom. He wanted to take another shower before he got into what she wanted to get into. He had to figure out this one. But when he got upstairs she had already made him a hot bath with candles and rose petals in the tub. She had lit incense in the bedroom. "Hi baby." She turned and smiled at him. "Hi Lon. What's all this?" "This is a glad your home welcome." "Really? Well maybe I should be gone every day all day." he laughed.

"No. I don't think so. We've been getting along so well I just wanted to show you how much I love you and am glad that we're working things out. Come on. Take those clothes off and get into this water." He stripped. He walked over to the tub and stepped in. "What you got on under that robe?" "Don't you even worry about that. You just sit back and relax and

I'll be right back." Lonnie went downstairs to fix Graham a plate of dinner. She loved him. She didn't know what was going on with her husband lately but their lovemaking and their time spent together was becoming more wonderful. He seemed to be getting his confidence back. She truly did adore him. She wanted her marriage to work and she decided she was going to trust him. At her Sister Friend club that she has weekly they even noticed a change in her. They told her she seemed a lot happier. They prayed for her that this would last and that God's will be done in her marriage. She had faith in God and in her husband. She got two glasses and the wine from the freezer. She juggled that and a plate of dinner for him. She was going to feed her man while he was in the tub. She had been planning it all day while she was at work. He wasn't home when she got home but that made it better for her to plan the evening. It was almost getting late before he showed up. She felt the edge coming back wondering where he was and what he was doing. She prayed about it. After she prayed she heard the door open. She prayed a silent Thank you Jesus and waited for her husband to come upstairs. He looked good as usual. He almost looked like he was hiding something but she thought her mind might've been playing a trick on her. Before he arrived she put on a new teddy that she had wanted to wear for him for months. There never was a right time but tonight was the night. She went into the bathroom and knelt on the floor. She poured two glasses of wine. She gave Graham his and picked up his plate. She fed him every bite. She ran more hot water and put in more bubbles for him. The scent of fresh vanilla musk filled the room. He looked good in that water with his gold earrings in his ears and gold around his neck. A gift she gave him last Christmas. "So when do I get to see what's under that robe woman?" "Patience baby. As soon as I dry you off." He was getting a little excited. She picked up the wine glasses and headed for the bedroom. After he lay on the bed she got hot oil and rubbed him down from shoulder to heel. He loved it. He turned over for her to do the front and she obliged. Making her way to his erection she rubbed it smoothly. He was so turned on. She stood over him and let her robe fall on the bed. He smiled. She was relieved. She had gained a couple of pounds but he obviously couldn't tell so she went with it. "Come here chocolate girl." He pulled her down on top of him. They made love and drank wine for hours. When the night was over and morning was nearing he went through the house with her and helped her blow out all the candles and to turn off the radio. Before they headed upstairs he grabbed a blanket from the closet and put it around her. He headed for the couch. They made love once again on the couch and slept there until they heard the delivery boy throw the newspaper at the door the next morning. Graham felt like the luckiest man alive. As he lay in bed watching her hustle off to work, he thought that soon he would have to start making some ends meet before this wonderful life turned sour again. He didn't want that. Maybe she was right. Maybe he should stop his get rich quick schemes and knuckle down and find another job. But he felt so close. This idea was too good to ignore. Many times he thought about the danger of his blackmailing Trace Reese and what could happen to him. But he felt like he wouldn't be one of those types of people that keep blackmailing you until they bled you dry. He wanted one big payday and he would never bother the woman again. At least that was his plan. Lonnie was a good woman. A fine woman. And she deserved better. He wanted himself to be that better person. He didn't want some other brother to enjoy all the fruits of what he had last night. *I better get it together* he thought. *I better get it together.* "Bye baby. I'm outta here." Lonnie left the house in a hurry. Graham decided to lie in bed a couple more hours and get some sleep. He didn't sleep too well on the couch last night. It seemed like a good idea at the time, but during the night he wish he hadn't. His back was killing him.

Chapter Thirteen

Graham woke up with fresh ideas of trying to get money from Trace Reese. He didn't want to involve anyone else in his plan because he didn't know whom he could trust and he also did not want to have to share his wealth. He had visions of living in a fine home with fine food and fine wine. He thought maybe he'd even get Lonnie a maid. Maybe they could adopt a baby since Lonnie couldn't have any. And with the money they'd have he was sure they could get a baby with money in the bank. He got himself ready to return to the neighborhood to seek out the apartment. He felt this might be the day. He would hate to have put all this time in and miss going over there one day. But after last night and being in that apartment he thought maybe no one would be there for a while. He had to see.

Trace got a call on her private line in her office that she needed to get over to her apartment because it might have been broken into. The only person to have this number was the landlord of the property and the apartment was listed under a different name. Trace was afraid to go over for fear of being recognized going there in public. She thought of calling Jeronn but didn't want to bother him with this. She didn't want to involve him in her business anymore than she had to. She got dressed and headed right over. When she got there nothing looked out of place. She couldn't tell anything was upset. There were a few notes left under the door. She had seen these before. Good riddens, she thought. She dusted the apartment and sat around for a while. She wasn't feeling depressed or anything so having a drink and lighting up a joint were the furthest things from her mind, even if they were her usual habits. She looked in the drawer by the bed and pulled out her old letters from Jeronn. She sometimes read them when she felt overwhelmingly lonely. Most times she cried after reading them. Trying to figure out how he could write such beautiful things and then leave her the way he did. The past couple of months with Jeronn just flew by and she felt like she was falling in love all over again. He was keeping something from her and she could tell, but she didn't know what. She packed a few things from the closet and sat them by the door. She didn't feel like staying long. She didn't really feel like being here anymore. She hadn't been back to this apartment for a while and she certainly didn't miss it. She checked the complete apartment before she decided to leave. Nothing was out of place. Before she left she packed a stash of weed in her suitcase as well, locked the door and left. She was thinking that pretty soon she was going to have to get rid of that place. Trace called a friend for lunch and spent the afternoon gossiping and shopping. Teresa was glad to hear from her. They hadn't talked in a long time and Trace was distancing herself. But to hear from her now was a good sign. Trace was skeptical about telling her about Jeronn. She was avoiding telling her for a long time. She knew this was a dearest friend and that she would be supportive, but ever since Jeronn left her all those years ago she would dog him out whenever she read something about him and Retha in any paper. But still, this was her friend and she had to tell her. "T, I have something to tell you and I don't know how to tell you?"

"What?"

"You probably already know and you're just making me sweat."

"If it's about Jeronn, yes I already know. I can read." "Yeah, it's about Jeronn."

"Mph. So, what's his story?"

"No story. We ran into each other, one thing leads to another and we've been dating again." "Dating? Honey, you gave that man the best years of your life. You're past dating. You're just bringing more drama in ya life?"

"No, I'm not bringing drama into my life. We barely talk about the old days. We don't even talk about the future. We just, talk."

"MM-Hmm."

"Teresa, don't do that. I need you girl. I need you to tell me to go for it. I need you to .." "What? Tell you he's not going to hurt you again? I can't tell you that T. Just like I can't tell you whether to be with him or not. And with that goofy smile on your face it seems you've already made up your mind." She glanced at her sideways. Trace smiled. "Don't be flashing them big old teeth at me. You know I don't like what you're doing? It's bad enough you disappear for days at a time and nobody can find you. Now with Jeronn back in the picture I'll probably never see you again. I'm surprised you called me today. What did he need a break? I'm surprised you can walk. He been laying on you day and night hasn't he?" Trace was laughing hysterically. Teresa always made her feel silly. They were silly together. They even had the same silly laugh. But she couldn't help it. She loved her. "Actually T, we haven't done anything."

"What? Hold the phone. Did you just say you've been seeing this man again all this time and you ain't gave him no coochie?"

"Ugh, Teresa why you gotta make it sound like that? No I haven't given him anything. And I don't intend to anytime soon. I'm not going out like that. I gave it up to him the first time we met and I couldn't even get him to marry me, I'm not doing that again. I don't even know where we're headed or if we're even headed anywhere." "You know what I say? I say you should gone head and hook up with Ross. That is one fine brother."

"He's also slipperier than a snake. I can't trust him. He's too easy. I mean, he's just too accessible or something. Besides, you never mix business with pleasure. RL's my agent and that's that. I never liked the fact that he has two last names. What the hell is a Ross Langley anyway?" They cracked up laughing.

"Yeah, but he's fine girl. He can have any sister he wants. I saw him checking you out at that Dolphins game. Girl he was checking out them jeans." "Shut up girl. I wasn't even trying to see that."

"Well, I did. I wish he would look at me the way he looks at you. My husband's so wrapped up with his golf tournament I can't even get none." "That's what you get for marrying a white man." She laughed. "See if you had've married a brother you'd be at home with sore lips right now." They laughed. "No you didn't. Oh no you didn't. Girl if I was married to a brother he wouldn't be wrapped up with golf, he'd be wrapped up with the remote control Okay?"

After lunch Trace called Jeronn on the phone and asked him to meet her for dinner. Of course he was more than happy to be there. Jeronn called up a friend of his to let him know he was going to be stopping over. When he got there his friend was more than happy to see him. Jeronn referred to him as an executive pimp. The front of his house was ghetto fabulous with three of the nicest rides sitting out front and 3 acres of greenery behind it. It was a multicolored brick house with 5 bedrooms, private baths in each room, a swimming pool in back big enough to play bumper pool in, and a double fireplace. It was tight. Jeronn knew how Red got all his money though. He got it being in the game. Jeronn never had any desire to be in the game of dealing drugs, but he certainly had a desire to do them. The problem was, once he started, sometimes it was hell trying to stop. It was another reason Retha left him. But tonight he was going to see Trace and he felt he needed the confidence to tell her all he needed to tell her before Ross Langley poisoned her mind with his own understanding. Red greeted him in the library. He was smooth as butter. There were three women sitting in their all having drinks and adoring Red. Just the way he liked it. Red handled his business. He didn't bother the police and they didn't bother him. As long as he was quiet and kept to himself, there was no need for anyone to bother him. Sometimes he would have dinner parties and invite his neighbors just to show them a side of himself, they never would expect. He often offered himself generously to whatever they needed. He supported their causes and he was respectable. The neighbors all thought he was an heir to a fortune. They never questioned. They never had a reason to. But Red knew what he was. He was a Millennium Pimp. His favorite saying was as a classic as his cars out front. "The hoes love me." But get him around some white people, you would never hear foul language come pass his lips. But the truth was the ladies did love him. Even the women who weren't just hanging around for what they could get. Red was a smooth brother. He was light skinned with green eyes and a sexy smile. He had a very light mustache. The kind you would expect Al Capone to wear. He was never a goatee man. His clothes were all tailor-made. Red was the man. Jeronn loved him like a brother. Red had a soft spot for Jeronn as well. Red wanted Jeronn to lay off the drugs. He told him drugs were what made Retha leave, not everything else. The fact was Retha did drugs as much as Jeronn, if not more. And she was always in Red's face. He knew Jeronn didn't love Retha the way he loved Trace, but he cared about her. After sharing a drink and catching up, Red knew why Jeronn was there. If Jeronn was there that meant he was feeling pretty low. "Jeronn. What can I do for you baby?"

"Man. I don't even know what to say."

"You sure you want to be here man?"

"Man, if I didn't need to be here I wouldn't?" "So what else can I do for you? I see you dating that fine Trace again." He displayed his hands at the women. As if to say they were his if he wanted. "Man some other time. I won't be staying long. I'm actually meeting Trace for dinner tonight." He sat down and stirred his drink with his finger. The women got up to leave. They knew what time it was when Red went to his bookshelf.

"How's that working out for you man?" He opened a book that was obviously hollow. "What can I say? It's peaches. It's just that she got this dude man, her agent. Hanging around her, snooping all up in our business, man. He walks around there like he player-player man." "Oh yeah? So they're doing the do or what?"

"Naw man, nothing like that. At least that's what she says. But I see the way she looks at him man. She used to look at me like that man. Until I hurt her."

"Man don't do that to yourself again. Don't even talk about it. That was years ago. Let it go. Yall kickin' it now so don't even worry about it." Jeronn did a couple of lines in front of Red. It was no biggie to him. Red didn't care either. All he asked was don't get all crazy around him, because he had no problem with turning a dude up dead. At least that's what he would tell people. But Jeronn was cool. He knew he would have no problems with Jeronn. After Jeronn did a couple of lines he was obviously more relaxed and looser with his tongue. He let his weakness show. Red was always telling him to protect himself. If he was going to have himself out there like that cover his ass. Red didn't want to see Jeronn like this if he was going to have dinner with Trace. He always wanted to see Trace and Jeronn get back together ever since he met Jeronn a few years ago. Jeronn was rolling back then. He had a booming house, a sexy wife and unlimited access. He remembered meeting him at a swank up in the mountains. Nothing but the elite was there and Jeronn and Red stuck out like sore thumbs. But they were smooth with it. They both happened to be in the Men's room at the same time. Jeronn was cooling off after having sent Retha to their room to lie down. She had obviously had too much to drink. Jeronn worked the room and they ended up talking. Jeronn noticed how the most beautiful women were always hanging around Red and he told him so. Red peeped him up on the real deal on why the women hung around. They were sprung on the white horse. Jeronn wanted some of the action and eventually he and Red became the closest friends. They were tight from then on. Red never told Jeronn, that after his divorce, Retha was over his house all the time trying to become his lady. He didn't have the heart. Retha wasn't his type anyway. She was too needy. But she certainly knew her way around the bedroom.

After they had caught up, Red asked Jeronn to invite Trace out to his home for a dinner party. He would send a limo to pick her up and they could all have dinner together tonight. Jeronn thought it was a cool idea and gave Trace a call. Red went to lay Jeronn out some dinner clothes. He knew Jeronn wouldn't have time to get home and get back.

Chapter Fourteen

"Chanelle, I will probably be in very late tonight so don't wait up."

"Are you still having dinner with Jeronn?" she asked. "Yes we're going to

have dinner at a friend of his. He's sending a limo to pick me up." "Oh a

limo. Well!! Have a good evening Miss Reese" she laughed and left the

room. Maja called up to tell her the limo had arrived. As she descended

the stairs she heard her private phone ringing and knew it had to be Ross.

She didn't have time for him right now. She didn't want to keep the limo

waiting. She'd been very excited when Jeronn asked her to have dinner

with a friend of his. She wanted to meet some of his friends. She wanted

to be a part of his life again. She wanted to know what he does with

himself. She told Maja that if Ross called, tell him that she was out for the

night and she would return his call tomorrow afternoon. She got in the

limo and headed into the night. Jeronn was very nervous all of a sudden

about her arrival. He was nervous that she might notice how nervous he

was. His palms were sweating. Red told him to calm down and have a

drink. He told him that he didn't need any more powder and to just relax

and chill. He had sent his lady friends away and had a very special lady

joining them for dinner. She was arriving just as Red sat to poor himself a

drink. Red greeted her at the door with flowers!! He always had fresh

flowers for whatever occasion he may need them. The women didn't seem to notice. They loved him anyway. "Jeronn, I'd like you to meet Mai. Mai this is my good friend Jeronn Clarke." "Jeronn Clarke?" she smiled. "Thee Jeronn Clarke. Producer?"

"The one and only." Jeronn smiled and kissed her hand. "Well Red, I see you do swing in different circles. Just when I think I know everything about you." "Well if you don't baby you will before the night is over." They smiled at each other, understanding his freaky undertones. "Mai is a very good friend of mine Jeronn. I met her in Hong Kong when I was there on some business. Shall I pour us all a drink?" "Will it just be the three of us?" Mai asked. "Don't get too excited Mai. Jeronn here is waiting on his ladylove to arrive any minute. Why don't we listen to some music while we wait for dinner." They all sat around talking about Jeronn's movies and his current affairs. Jeronn was more nervous than ever. He started wondering if Trace would realize Red is more than just a good friend. He knew he was becoming paranoid but he felt helpless to stop it. Part of him wanted to get high more and another part of him didn't want to give himself away to Trace. Trace arrived and Red headed for the door. He leaned over to Jeronn and told him to relax. Jeronn took a handkerchief and wiped the sweat from his brow and sat nervously waiting for Trace to come in. Red met her at the door with oozing charm and hidden attraction. Trace was stunning in a lime colored one peace halter dress that revealed the curves of her hips. She wore it well. Red was aching inside. He didn't realize she'd be so beautiful in person. Whenever he'd seen her on television he'd wonder what it would be like to have a woman like that as his own. He had plenty of women but none with style and class like this woman. Trace was the kind of woman you married and he knew that from jump. She was fine as wine and smooth as chocolate.

She stood there with her hand out for what seemed like an eternity as she waited for whomever this gentleman was to stop daydreaming and take her hand. "Oh. I'm so sorry. I was just thinking what a lovely vision you are." She smiled sweetly. "Well, thank you. And you are..."

"Oh I'm sorry. I'm a very good friend of Jeronn's. We're like brothers you could say." "Oh really? Well that's nice. And where is Mr. Clarke?"

"Excuse me?" "I'm sorry. Where is Jeronn?"

"Oh, well he's right through these doors. Why don't I show you the way?"

"Thank you. But you still didn't tell me your name?" "Oh well, my friends call me Red. I would be honored if you would do the same Miss Reese." "Well if I'm going to call you Red then you must call me T."

"You got it T." He smiled as he licked his lips and admired the view. She knew he was flirting. It was very obvious. But she was used to it. She never paid much attention to harmless flirting. It went with the territory.

And if he and Jeronn were close like brothers as he said, she knew she shouldn't put much stock in what he was doing. Although, he was fine. Mighty fine. As they entered the room, Jeronn stood up and greeted her with a soft kiss on the cheek. She held his hand and was very happy to see him. He looked exceptionally good tonight. He smelled wonderful. She wore one of her sexiest dresses hoping tonight would be the night.

He poured her a drink and sat down next to her. He couldn't take his eyes off her. She was breathtaking. Red made the introductions to Mai and they waited for the chef to tell them that dinner was served. They continued their conversation of politics and music and reminisced about the old days. Trace told Red and Mai about her daughter and granddaughter. Red complimented her by expressing how terribly young she looked to be a grandmother. At dinner Jeronn noticed how much Red was enjoying Trace and barely paying attention to Mai. At first he thought maybe he was being paranoid, but the look on Mai's face showed she noticed it too. Trace took no notice. She was used to being the center of attention. She never failed to capture a room. Even the smallest audience. Jeronn and Trace held hands across the table and shared longing glances. It was either the atmosphere or the wine or both, but they both felt the electricity. Trace thought tonight might actually be the night. She couldn't wait until dinner was over so they could drive back to his place and consummate their affections. Red interrupted their eye dance.

"So T, would you and Jeronn like to stay for a night cap? I thought we could all take a dip in the Jacuzzi after dinner." *'T? Where did that come from calling her T?'* Jeronn thought. He thought maybe he was just tripping. Red wouldn't dare over step that way. "Oh well, uh..actually I have an early start in the morning and I thought I would just head on home." "Aw, come on T. Tomorrow's Sunday. Can't whatever it is you have to do wait until the afternoon?" He was smooth, she thought. "MM. Well, I guess it could. I am the boss." she smiled at him. "That's what I thought." he tipped his glass to her. *'What in the hell is going on here?'* Jeronn thought. *Are they just going to sit here and flirt right in front of me. And nobody asked me what I thought about staying the night.*

"Well I guess if that's what my baby wants to do then that's what we'll do." he smiled at her. "I'm afraid though I haven't brought a bathing suit." "Oh that's okay. I have everything you need." Mai rose from the table. "I'll show you where they are. We can go ahead of the guys and relax and talk awhile. Okay?" Trace got up from the table and headed off with Mai. Mai turned around to Red. "Don't be long baby."

"I can't help it. I was born that way." He said it to Mai, but its intention was to let Trace know. While they were gone Jeronn asked Red was he coming on to Trace. Red told Jeronn he was being ridiculous and to chill out.

"So Trace, how long have you and Jeronn been dating?" Mai asked. "Oh well. We have a long history. But we've only been seeing each other again seriously for a couple of months." "Again? You've dated before?" "Yes. We dated for some years before we split up. We moved out here and things changed. The rest is history. But we've started seeing each other again and that's what's up with us. So tell me. What's up with you and Red? How long have you been dating?" "Oh Red and I aren't dating. We just get together sometime to how do you American's say? Get jiggy with it?" "Oh. Well, hm..What can I say to that? I ain't mad at ya." "Oh don't worry. There's nothing to say. You couldn't possibly think he'd be a man of mine with all that shameless flirting he was doing down there." "Well I was wondering how come you weren't saying anything." "Oh Red and I have an understanding. I really like him though. But in my country I could never date a man like Red. My father would be shamed." "Oh. I see. Well, I guess we better get downstairs." "Wait a minute." She walked over to Trace. She put her hand up to her face gently. "If you ever want to experience something different, feel free to look me up." She let her finger slide down to Trace' breast before smiling and leaving the room. Trace stood there stunned. She played it off and got her butt downstairs real quick. She couldn't wait to tell Jeronn what had happened. They sat in the Whirlpool and drank wine and laughed. A few times Trace could have sworn she felt Red's foot caress her own. She also thought she felt Mai's foot glide down her leg. And of course Jeronn's. His caress was unmistakable. Maybe because it was the only leg she was interested in. You would think after the things she had been doing for the past couple of years that she would not be fazed by the absolute kinkiness of the situation she was in, but she was. She burst out laughing at the thought of it. Here she was in a whirlpool with the love of her life, a guy she just met and his bi-sexual lover and all three of them wanted to have sex with her. It was the funniest situation she had ever found herself in. Oddly enough, everybody in the whirlpool realized it too. But this is where Jeronn felt his confidence. He knew that he would be the only one loving her tonight. It's not the place where he wanted their first time together again to be, but it would have to be. He had to get closer to her before his whole life changed. He hadn't forgotten about Ross Langley. He definitely wasn't about to let that brother have her. And Red oozing sex and money since the minute she walked in the door. He knew he had to get the ball rolling. He pulled Trace in front of him and asked her if she were ready to go upstairs. She smiled and told him she absolutely was. He held her hand and led her out of the whirlpool. Red and Mai stayed in the whirlpool a little while. Besides it was their favorite place to make love anyway. As soon as Trace closed the bedroom door, Jeronn was on her. He held her and kissed her deeply. She could feel him rising. It made her warm inside. Jeronn led her to the bed and peeled off her bikini. Her body was just as beautiful as he remembered it. She felt soft and creamy all over. He cupped her breasts and held them on each side of his face while he sucked wet kisses all over her body. She held his head close to her. She could never resist him. He was her king. And he made her feel like a queen. He laid her down on the bed and lifted her thigh to his face. He sucked her inner thigh from her crotch to her knee and she loved it. She squeezed along his head and his shoulders frantically. She couldn't get enough. It was on. She wrapped both of her legs around his shoulders and moved until she couldn't take it anymore. They were both as freaky as they used to be. It was better than before. As he entered her, she closed her eyes and pulled him deeper. She wanted his lovemaking to wash away all the years of pain she felt without him. She caressed him deeply while washing away the rush of hurt she had held inside for all these years. She still loved him so very much. She loved his moves. She loved his smell. She loved his touch. They were all over each other. They made love over and over until they were exhausted. They were breathless and speechless. They lay there holding each other. There was so much to say and nothing at all to say. Trace could hear Jeronn drifting off into sleep and decided to find her way to the kitchen for some ice water. She often drank ice water in the middle of the night after drinking wine all evening. She put on a robe and made her way down the stairs. There was a soft light coming from the room they had been in earlier so she headed off in the other direction towards the kitchen. After going through the swinging doors she turned on the light and tried to find the glasses. After getting her water she turned to leave the room and found Red standing there eyeing her. He was wearing red silk boxers and nothing else. He was carrying a glass of wine and had a towel hanging over his shoulders. His body was perfect. He had muscular arms and she could see the huge veins underneath his skin. She could hear her heartbeat. He smiled at her and turned to the side so she could walk past. She ducked beneath his arm and headed for the stairs. "I love the smell of a woman after making love. It's the most erotic scent in the world." She turned and looked at him. Her ice broke her silence. "Red, although I'm flattered at your obvious attempt to seduce me, I'm in love with Jeronn and I don't foresee anything at all happening between us." He glided across the room and stood over her. "T..mph. Listen baby, the furthest thing from my mind is seducing you. Before this whole chemistry between us is through you'll be begging me for it baby." She licked her lips. She opened her mouth to speak, but she couldn't.

Before she could, he licked his finger and parted her robe and inserted it inside her vagina. She let him. It felt good. He rubbed her clit gently and flicked it. He took his fingers out and rubbed his fingers on his chest. Before either of them spoke, Mai poked her head out of the room. "Are you coming back daddy?" "Be right there Mai," he answered without turning around. Trace fixed her robe and went up the stairs. His arrogance was too much for her, but it certainly made her hot. Where did this man come from? She slept lightly that night.

Early the next morning, she woke Jeronn and told him she wanted to leave. She didn't want to run into Red. Jeronn tried to talk her into staying for breakfast but she was adamant about leaving. She showered and redressed in her halter dress. Jeronn waited for her down stairs. He was in the library talking with Red from what she could hear. Apparently he and Mai spent the night in there. She opened the front door and headed for the limo. She heard Jeronn and Red talking behind her. She didn't dare turn around. After getting in the car she saw Jeronn headed behind her with Red in tow. She turned straight ahead and waited for Jeronn. He climbed in on the other side. The driver let her window down when he saw Red coming and Red leaned in to talk to them. "So Jeronn I guess I'll see you next weekend brother." "Yeah man. See you next weekend."

"Trace, I hope I can count on you to come to my party next weekend. I'm sure your presence will be missed if you weren't here."

"I-I don't know. I'll have to check my schedule. I think my agent has me quite busy these days. It's a wonder I was able to make it out last night."

"Well. I'll just keep my fingers crossed until then." He held out the same two fingers that he had stuck between her legs last night. She noticed. He kissed his fingers and bid them good-bye. Trace was smitten. But her love for Jeronn would rule.

Chapter Fifteen

Graham left a note under Trace's apartment door. He thought for sure that would get her attention. He had no idea when she would find it but he thought it shouldn't be long. In the meantime he would spend time at home with his wife. He just hoped that the peaceful time they had could remain that way. He knew he couldn't keep hanging out around that apartment. He hadn't seen anyone going in there for weeks. He just had to be patient. His hunches had rarely been wrong before.

Trace spent the next couple of days working and thinking about Red. She knew there was some chemistry between them, but she also knew it was only sex. She had been that route before. She wanted love. She wanted the love that she and Jeronn used to share. She knew they could be that way again. This past weekend proved it. Jeronn was all over her. It was wonderful. She hadn't felt that way about sex in a long time. She felt wanted and desired and loved. Jeronn was all man. The way he whispered her name when they made love made her body tingle. She sat on the phone the next day telling Teresa all about her weekend with Jeronn and what happened with Red. She couldn't believe it. They cracked up laughing for an hour before Trace had to get off the phone. Ross was coming over to go over some things with her. She had some papers to sign

or something. Just as she was hanging up, she got a beep on her call

waiting. It was Jeronn asking if he could come over. He needed to talk to

her. She told him sure and he said he'd be over with Chinese food and

they could have dinner and talk. She couldn't wait to see him. She put on

some peach Capri pants and a peach blouse to match. She was feeling

cool and casual. The Miami heat was sweltering. Just as she was

reapplying her make up Maja came to inform her that Ross was downstairs

in her study. She headed on down to get the business over with so she

could prepare for her visit with Jeronn. Maybe they'd go for a ride in her

convertible after dinner. She needed to talk to him as well. Ross was

looking pleased and handsome sitting in her chair. He had on white pants

and a white shirt with the sleeves rolled up. He had on leather sandals and

sunglasses. He rarely dressed this casual. "So Mr. Langley, what is it I

can do for you today?" She greeted him with a smile and came over to

hug him. They are usually good friends, she hoped her relationship with

Jeronn wouldn't change that. "Well, Miss T," he smiled. "I was hoping I

could go over an itinerary with you for your engagements for the next

couple of months." "Okay, shoot. Let's have a look at it." He handed her

the appointments. She did her usual. Crossed out engagements she didn't

want to do in red and put blue question marks by the ones she wanted to think about. Anything she didn't touch was a definite appointment. Ross was used to the routine. He looked over the papers. "So then Oprah's a go then?" "Yeah, I thought it would be nice to go and visit my family while I'm there. I haven't been to Chicago in awhile." "Okay Great! Now on another topic, what do you say about you and I having dinner together tonight?" "Well Ross. I'm sorry I can't join you tonight. I think I'm just going to stay in tonight. But thank you for the invite." Ross cleared his throat.

"Well okay Trace, but there are some things I would like to discuss with you." She knew what was coming.

"What is it Ross. Is it more of your ideas about Jeronn because I truly don't want to hear them." "Trace seriously boo, what do you really know about the man? I mean I have known you for some years now and Jeronn just doesn't seem like the type of character that a person like you should be associated with." "Ross you don't know a damned thing about Jeronn. He's known me for years too. Intimately. I was going to marry the man remember? And if you think that Jeronn is not the type of man that I would want in my life then the truth is you don't know me after all these years anyway."

"Trace, I'm telling you this for your own good. Jeronn isn't like the man you used to know. He's had some dealings with some bad people. Rough people."

"Well you know what? Let me just find all that out by myself okay? Let Jeronn tell me." "I'm trying to tell you before you get sucked into something you can't get out of. Trace, I care about you and I always have. I just want what's best for you and your career!"

"Ross, you know and I know you care about me. But I think Jeronn knows a little bit more about me than you do and I don't think he would hurt me. Whatever trouble he's gotten himself into, whenever he's ready to tell me about it he will. We've already discussed it anyway. He has something he wants to discuss with me and I believe that whatever he's going through he's ready to tell me about it."

"So I take it he's coming over tonight?" "Well as a matter of fact he is." "So when you said you just wanted to be at home alone tonight you meant with him." "I never said alone, but yes he's coming over later and we're going to have a little dinner and talk. Now if you're through with the inquisition Ross I'd like to relax awhile before he gets here."

"Trace, please be careful. You have no idea what his life has been like since you've been out of touch."

"And I suppose you do? You have no idea what my life has been like without him. You only see Trace Reese the celebrity, the singer, because that's all I let you see, but you don't know Trace the woman. Trace the..Never mind. Ross please don't overstep here. You're my agent and a

good friend. Let's not ruin that by forgetting who pays who okay?"

Ross stood up to leave. He picked up the folder and exited her office. She

hated speaking to him that way but she hated when anyone tried to make

her do what she didn't want to do. She sat down on the sofa and stared at

the ceiling. Tonight was the night she was going to tell him that she was

getting rid of her apartment. She was going to ask him to help her pack

her things so that she wouldn't have to trust anyone else to it. She knew it

would make him happy and she couldn't wait to tell him. She couldn't stop

thinking about the things that Ross said to her about Jeronn. She knew he

knew something, but she would rather hear it from Jeronn. She had

learned a long time ago not to listen to any information second hand.

Especially since someone was always printing something about her. Trace

drifted off into a light sleep waiting for Jeronn to arrive.

Hey baby glad you could make it. Let me take that bag from you. I've

been thinking about you all day. I couldn't wait for you to hold me in your

arms. She ripped the shirt from his muscular chest, placing hot kisses all

over his body. She reached down to unbuckle his pants. She looked up to

stare into his eyes. It was Red. Her clothes disappeared. They made love

on the carpet. Fast and furiously. He pulled her hair so hard but she

didn't care. She loved it this way. He made her feel tingly all over. He turned her over and repeated her name..Trace...baby...Trace...Trace...

She woke up. Jeronn was standing over her calling her name. "Trace baby wake up. You're dreaming. You were whimpering baby. Was it a bad dream?" Trace put her hand to her forehead and looked around. It was too real. She had dreamed that she and Red were in this very room and it wasn't real. She smiled up at Jeronn and gave him the biggest hug. "Where's the food?" "It's in the kitchen." "Well, let me go and wash up and I'll be right back to join you okay?" "Okay sweetie. Are you sure you're okay. You sounded pretty excited in your sleep?"

"Oh, I don't even remember what I was dreaming about" she lied. She smiled and left the room. *"What up with that?'* she thought. Jeronn went to the kitchen to prepare their dinner. He thought they could have dinner on the loggia and he would finally tell her everything about himself. They ate and drank slowly and finally they both felt it was time to talk. Trace went first. "Jeronn I have something I've been wanting to tell you." "Really? What is it baby?" he was chewing on sprout. "Well, I've decided to give up my apartment." she blurted. "I've been having a change of life and I've been doing a lot of soul searching and the truth is now that you're back in my life, I cannot consciously justify why I would ever go back there. Sure I would love to still keep it just for sanities sake, but I feel like it's time. I've been thinking that I would take a chance on love again and hope for the best." Jeronn didn't speak. "Jeronn, I hope I'm not reading too much into this relationship. I mean I do hope that we're on the same page." "Oh yeah. Baby of course we are. I'm sorry I didn't say anything. My mind was just thinking back well you know. Anyway, I think that's a wonderful idea. I think that's the best news I've heard in a long time." Trace picked up her wine glass. "Here's to new beginnings." He shared her toast. Well, Jeronn, I believe it's your turn. Was there something you wanted to tell me?" "Well, I don't actually know where to begin. I mean you know, so much has happened."

"Well why don't you start at the last likely place to start and work your way back. That works for me sometimes."

"Okay, well here goes. I haven't been at the top of my game lately. My career is not as hot as it used to be and the truth is it's all my fault."

"So what happened?"

"Well, let's see. First, Retha happened. I can't totally blame her for everything, but she was a major part. I put so much into getting her career off the ground that I couldn't see the road ahead. I made some bad business decisions and it basically bankrupted me. I've taken out loans from people and haven't made good on my commitments and the truth is I'm finding myself in a lot of trouble. I didn't want to tell you about this a couple of months ago when we started seeing each other again, because you weren't in a good place in your life and for two I didn't want you to think that the feelings I have for you, were only due to your money. Not that I would ever ask you for money. I know that that would take a lot of nerve to do something like that especially with our history, but I wasn't ready to tell you at the time." "Well Jeronn, if that's what you wanted to tell me then let me tell you this. I don't think that problem is so great that God and we can't handle it together. We'll just pay back what you owe, put you in touch with some of the right people and get your career back on. Get it the way it should be."

"No Trace, I can't accept that from you."

"Honey don't take it that way. A long time ago, you put an investment in my career and this is my way of returning the favor. Trust me I'll be getting something out of it," she laughed. "Trace, I don't know what to say. I really don't. I'm sorry that I took so long to tell you that. But there is more that you need to know."

"More? Like what?"

"Well, that day that I came to your apartment." he hesitated. "Well?" she looked into the sunset.

"Well, I had the wrong apartment. I ended up at your place totally by accident." She turned slowly to look in his eyes. "I don't know how it happened but there I was. When I heard your voice behind the door I started to walk away. But sheer curiosity made me stand there to see if the voice I heard was really yours. I couldn't walk away. And when you started going off about me coming to see a whore and cheating on Retha I never really commented because that's not what I was doing at all. I never said anything because I didn't want you to be embarrassed." Tears rolled down her face. She couldn't believe what she was hearing. She felt so ashamed. At first she had considered the way they were reunited as fate, but this wasn't funny at all. It was totally humiliating. She stared at nothing. She always dreaded anyone finding out her secret on purpose. But for the man she loved, who had left her for another woman, to find out this way? She couldn't face him. She turned her back to him. He put his hands on her shoulders. She pulled away.

"Trace, I'm so sorry. I wanted to tell you but I didn't know how. I didn't mean to hurt you. Baby I really didn't."

"I know Jeronn. It's not your fault. It's just that sometimes when I think of the way my life has turned out and the way other people see me and the way that I know that I really am, I feel like such a fool. I feel like a hypocrite. And now to know that when you came to that apartment you weren't even looking for what I thought you were looking for. I'm so embarrassed. You found me in that place acting like a fool. You must have thought I was a joke."

"No Trace. I didn't think anything bad about you. I thought to myself, what has happened to this woman to make her think that this road is a safe road? Or to make you think that life is no better than this. Trace I fully take the blame for all the wrong in your life. I know I'm responsible for it."

"Jeronn, I'm responsible for my own actions. I'm not a fool."

"You're right. You're not. We all make mistakes. Which is why if I'm going to be completely honest with you, I need to tell you what I was really doing there." Trace turned to face him. Her tear stained cheek streaked with mascara. He sighed deeply. "Trace I was there getting drugs." "What? I don't understand. You sell drugs?"

"No, not exactly."

"Then what exactly?"

"Well exactly, I've been doing drugs. I know that sounds stupid. Hell it sounds stupid now that I've said it out loud." Trace was speechless. "Now I feel embarrassed. And I know that all those times you heard me talking about people who did drugs and now here I am telling you, I'm just as weak as they are." "Jeronn? What am I supposed to say?"

"I don't know man. I don't even know what to say myself. I mean, hey. What can I say?" "So you're telling me that you're broke, your career is failing, you owe all kinds of money and you're on drugs? Don't you think drugs are the reason that all these things are happening to you? Or are you

not doing them as bad as you make it sound? I mean tell me what's up."

"I don't know what to say. I mean it's off and on. Sometimes when I feel

really bad I do it. Sometimes when I'm feeling good I use it. Sometimes I

just don't even bother with it. I mean I don't have to do it. I can definitely

go without it."

"Jeronn, what type of drugs are you using?"

He sighed. "Coke."

"Cocaine? And what you snort it? Smoke it? What?"

"Nall. Hell nall. I snort it."

"What? Man, I don't wanna hear anymore of this. Are you going to get

some help or stop or what?"

"I don't need any help. Do I look like I need help to you?"

"It doesn't matter what you look like. I know enough to know that if you

do it for any occasion you need some help."

"What occasion?"

"Jeronn you just told me that you do it if you're happy or sad, so if you do

it every time the wind blows you need some help."

"I don't know maybe I do need help."

"So you can come into my life and tell me I need counseling for my

emotions and what drives me to live a reckless life, but you can't get help for what's obviously destroying your life and your career." Trace left the room. She didn't want to hear anymore. She loved Jeronn but this is not something she wanted to hear. She thought about how far she's come in her career without Jeronn. She thought about how she had hoped all her dreams would come true with Jeronn, but when he left her he took her heart. And now knowing the shambles he's made of his life she just didn't think she could think of anything else right now. She got into her car and left him there. She didn't know where she was going but she couldn't stay there. She drove around for an hour before she found herself in front of her apartment. She contemplated going up there. She hadn't been there in a long time and she felt tortured about going up there now. Many times she's sat in her car trying to force herself not to go up there. Many times she couldn't help herself because of the solace she knew she would find behind that door. Knowing that no one would bother her there. She parked her car in the lower garage and headed up there. Her hand was trembling as she put the key in the lock. As she entered the apartment she stepped over a stack of notes left under her door. She tapped the lamp to turn it on and turned around to retrieve the notes. She looked them over and tossed them in the trash. She had no intention of returning any calls to any one. That life was behind her. She fell down on the sofa and hit the answering machine. She had twenty-two messages. All from the same people, all saying the same thing. Only a handful of people had this

private number, so she knew what it was all about. Den had called five

times. He could be so crass. She especially wasn't going to call him back.

She would just stay here and lay low for a couple of days. She knew she

would need food so she would call the market in the morning and have

some things sent over. She took a bath and sat back down on the couch

and grabbed the remote. She flipped on the television and sat watching

anything that was on. Her mind was tired from thinking about Jeronn and

his drugs. He knew how she felt about him doing drugs because he knew

what her mom had gone through to get off of drugs. It wasn't something

she was ready to commit to helping with. Hadn't he left her when she

needed him the most? And now while she was going through her own

ordeal, he dumped his drugs in her lap and his empty pockets. They were

both in bad situations, but Trace wasn't about to be his support right now.

She loved him, but she knew deep down she couldn't handle it. In the

past, she would have stuck by his side like glue to help him through it.

She figured he wouldn't come here looking for her because she had told

him that she was going to move out of this place. This is the last place he'd

look anyway. Besides, she thought, she was only going to be here a

couple of days. Maybe less. She might just go to Chicago earlier than

expected. She had the television down low and she thought she heard

172

someone in the hall downstairs. She muted the television so she could hear better. Someone was definitely coming up the stairs. She stayed quiet. She went over to peek through the hole to see if it were Jeronn. *He's smarter than I thought* she smiled. But when she looked out the hole, she didn't recognize the face. It wasn't Jeronn at all. And it wasn't one of her old friends. She didn't know who that man was. He stood by her door listening. She stood there watching him listen. She quietly backed away from the door and went into her bureau. She pulled out her automatic handgun and crept closer to the door. She peeked out. She noticed the man walking back down the stairs and she watched him. She waited. He left the building. She went over to the window and she watched him leave down the street. She wanted to call the police, but then she didn't want any recognition of her apartment in this neighborhood. It was a quiet neighborhood. Maybe Jeronn sent someone over here to look for her. She thought that had to be it. So she sat on the couch with her handgun in her lap and the TV muted and fell asleep. She awoke to a light knock on the door. She crept quietly over to the door. It was Dennis. She didn't really feel like being bothered, but she didn't feel like being jumpy all night either. "Just a minute," she sang. She went into her bedroom and put on her wig. She sprayed some cheap perfume in the air and put on a satin gown. She looked at herself in the mirror wondering what in the world she was doing. She knew this was wrong. But she really didn't want to be alone. She turned on the stereo and opened the door for Den. She gave him half a smile and pulled her hair closer to her face. "Always sitting in the dark aren't you Miriam?" "You know me. So what brings you over here this time of night? It's pretty late."

"I think you know what brings me here. Why don't you fix me a drink baby?" She was not in the mood for him tonight. She was thinking of Jeronn. She poured him a brandy and he lit a cigar. If she was going to be Miriam, she may as well get into the role. She poured herself a drink as well. She applied some horrible peach lipstick and brought in the drinks. By the time she turned around Den was out of his clothes and sitting buck-naked with his ashy ass on her leather sofa. "Why don't we go into the bedroom baby?"

"Sure. But why don't you give me a reason to go in the bedroom." His penis was standing straight up like a missile preparing for launch. With nothing to light the room, but the flashing lights on the stereo she knelt down in front of him and gave him what he wanted. His moaning was partially turning her on and partially making her sick. She grabbed his hand and led him to her room. After putting a condom on him, she laid on the bed. "Naw baby. You know how Den like it." She had almost forgotten. She laid him down and climbed on. He untied her satin gown and draped it on her sides. His pleasure was making her want to heave. She started moaning. This really got him off. He squeezed her breasts so hard she wanted to slap the hell out of him. But she wasn't Trace, she was Miriam. And Miriam didn't want anyone to know she was Trace. After it was over, Den went on and on about her not being around in a long time. Boring her to death with stories of his latest acquisition. She didn't really care, but she knew Dennis would stay with her tonight. Sometimes Dennis would bring her expensive gifts, which she kept in a safe. She went and poured Dennis another drink. After letting him screw her again, they fell asleep.

Chapter Sixteen

Jeronn woke up at four am worried out of his mind for Trace. She had walked out and never came back. He called her a few times, but she never answered. Neither did she answer her cellular phone. He figured he knew where she was and decided to take a ride. When he pulled in front of her place it was dark. He didn't see her car, but he knew there was a garage. Outside the apartment he didn't hear anything. He knocked softly but there was no answer. He pressed his ear to the door and heard the stereo. She was there. He knocked a few more times to no avail. He broke the lock. He noticed two glasses on the end table and caught his breath. *She wouldn't.* He thought. He raced to the bedroom and stood in the door. There she was. Asleep on the bed, wearing a ridiculous wig, with some fool on the bed snoring like a lawn mower. He was pissed. He flicked on the light and looked around. Neither of them stirred. After noticing two condom rappers on the floor he thought his heart would leap out of his chest. He couldn't catch his breath. He stood there shocked not knowing what to do. His mind was racing. Should he whoop her ass or just kill him. Before he could think of anything, Trace turned over and saw him standing there. She was horrified. How ridiculous she must look wearing the wig and lying there next to Den. She stared at Jeronn and woke Den up. "What? What the hell is going on?"

"Den. Just get your things and get out of here. Don't say a word."

"Miriam who the hell is this man? How did he get in?"

"Den, just get your stuff and get out of here." Jeronn was getting angrier by the second. This half naked man was questioning who he was and sleeping with his woman! He was seething. Trace jumped out of the bed and grabbed the sheet around her. She pulled Jeronn into the bathroom to talk to him. She begged him not to do anything. She pleaded for him not to hurt Den. She told him Den was an old friend and meant nothing to her.

"So that's it? You don't like something I say and you immediately go screw somebody else? Just like that? And what's with this ugly, blonde ass wig? Is that what this disappearance is all about? I'm sitting at home going out of my mind worried about you and you sleeping like a baby, letting this nigga screw you all night?"

"Jeronn please don't do this," she cried. "It's not like that."

"I know exactly how it is. Man, get your damn hands off me! I can't believe I was worried about yo' black ass all night." He stormed out of the bathroom. Den was long gone. Jeronn slammed and threw things around all over the house. Trace sat on her bed and cried. She dressed in a t-shirt and shorts and tried to calm him down. "And what the hell is this Miriam shit? Why is he calling you Miriam?"

"Jeronn, you don't think I would tell anybody my real name do you? You know I can't do that."

"I thought you were giving this up. You said you were giving up this apartment and this life. You don't have any reason to be here." He felt like screaming. Trace sensed it. Jeronn poured himself a drink. He threw the glass across the room.

"You wanna screw somebody else huh? Here." He grabbed her arm and pulled her in the bedroom.

"Take this crap off!" he yelled. "Jeronn don't you dare! Don't do this."

"You didn't tell old dude not to do it. Take your clothes off before I rip them off."

"Jeronn please!"

"Trace." She cried and pleaded. She could tell he was hurting. He looked crazed. He snatched her across the bed and ripped her t-shirt off. She tried to grab the sheet around her. "Oh hell no. You giving it up to me the same way you gave it up to him."

"Jeronn. Don't do this," she yelled. "So what you gone rape me now? Is that what you're planning to do? Are you high now?"

"Don't even try it. I'm giving you what you obviously want. I guess me telling you about my little drug problem was just too much for you. You couldn't handle it huh Trace? Well let me just give you what you can seem to handle."

"Jeronn please!" she begged. He was inside her. He was forcing himself inside her. She tried to put herself in a different frame of mind so it wouldn't hurt so badly but it was no use. She felt sick about what he saw her doing. He was hurt. She loved him. Right now they both hurt together. She cried. She felt humiliated. He didn't even finish. He just got up and stood in the doorway out of breath. He looked like he wanted to cry.

"You don't ever have to worry about seeing me again. I can't believe you did this." He was gone. Her heart ached. She cried for hours before falling to sleep.

The heat woke her out of her a deep dream. She returned her gun to the bureau and took a shower. She sat on the bed and thought about earlier that morning. She cried about Jeronn. When she could cry no more she called the market and ordered some cleaning supplies and groceries. She needed to clean up the mess Jeronn made. He had destroyed a couple of lamps and broke several glasses. She felt better about being here. She couldn't have sorted this out at home with Chanelle and Maja being there. She liked the quiet and the solitude. She needed it. She hadn't had it in awhile since she and Jeronn got back together but it felt good. After her food and supplies arrived, she found another stash of weed in her underwear drawer and decided she would have it later. She hadn't had that in awhile either. Just with Dennis last night. Her thoughts led to Jeronn and his drug problem. She opened the drapes wide and stared out into the neighborhood. There wasn't much to see. There was a woman walking her dog. There was a jogger across the way on a trail. Nothing much else. She remembered the man from last night and decided if there were anything to worry about she'd know it by now. She daydreamed about the dream she had yesterday before Jeronn came over. The dream of Red. She thought about calling him. But for what, she thought? *What could I possibly have to talk to him about? Jerron's drug problem? Was Red to blame?* After last night, she didn't want to have anything else to do with any man. Maybe not even Jeronn. But she couldn't help that her body was getting warm just thinking about Red. She decided to call Teresa. She blocked her number before calling so Teresa wouldn't know where she was calling from. Teresa was too nosey. They decided to meet in the city at a small cafe that they each loved. Once they got there Trace told Teresa all about Jeronn and his little problem. "Girl you got to be lying!"

"Girl I wish I was."

"So what did you tell him" "What could I tell him? Girl I left."

"You left him in your house?"

"Mm-hmm." "Girl are you crazy? The man just told you he was a drug addict and he ain't got no money and you leave him at home with all your nice stuff?" "T please. He's not going to touch any of my things. He wouldn't. Besides, Maja and Chanelle were there."

She lied. "So what happened when you got back what did he say?"

"Well..he was gone. When I got home he was gone." She lied again.

"Did you call him?" "Nope. I really don't want to talk to him. Which is why I called you." She said changing the subject. "I thought we could do something fun tonight. I have to leave for Chicago and I thought we could have some fun before I go. Let's go to the Marina. We can take a boat out there."

"You feel like dancing tonight girl?"

"Girl yes. I feel like some Salsa and Merengue and anything that'll get me moving these big hips girl!"

"Well let's go somewhere low key tonight girl. I don't feel like you spending the whole night signing autographs okay. I'm sorry, I know that's your job, but it can be a real pain in the butt."

"You're telling me!! Girl let's just take a boat and go over to that club off the island okay?" "Great. So do you want to go home and change or what?"

"Girl no. I do not want to go home, let's just go shopping and go back to your place."

"Okay cool." They spent the whole day shopping and talking about men. Trace eventually did have to sign a few autographs, but it wasn't too bad. Most people worked during the week anyway. Trace's cellular phone had been going off all day and she knew it might be Jeronn, but she just didn't feel like talking. Besides the fact that he was hurt, he hurt her more by forcing himself on her. Oddly enough, she wasn't as mad as she knew she should be. She called Chanelle to make sure everything was all right and told her about her plans. Chanelle had told her that Jeronn had called her a few times already but that was all he said. Trace told her she loved her and gave her the itinerary for the next few days. She would be spending some time with Teresa and then off to Chicago. But don't mention it to Jeronn. She left messages for Ross in case he called and that was it. Trace knew Jeronn was calling her cell phone, but he was blocking his number so she didn't answer it. Out on the boat it was a little chilly, but she was fine. After a few Tequilas the night was hot as July in Arizona. Tonight, she didn't care. When they got to the club Trace didn't have to wait in line with everyone else. That was a welcome perk to being a celebrity. A few men asked if they could come in the club with her as her guests, but she wasn't buying it. She smiled at them and waved and told them she'd see them inside and that was that. She was ushered to a nice table in back and prayed for no attention tonight. She wanted to drink and act a fool. Things like that were close to impossible when everyone knew your face. After they ordered their drinks the owner came over and asked if she'd like to join the V.I.P. room private party to avoid the crowd and she kissed his cheek and told him to lead the way. He apologized for his staff not being on their toes and ordered a complimentary bottle of the best champagne in the house. After finishing a bottle of Champagne Trace was feeling relaxed and wonderful. She went to the ladies room. As she was coming out she could have sworn she saw Red across the room. She thought her mind must have been playing tricks on her. Maybe she had too much to drink. She sat down with Teresa and told her all about Red. She didn't want to tell her but what could she do? Red might be here and she wanted to see him. They got up from their table and walked over to the one-way mirror to look out at the people on the dance floor. Trace turned to look around and she saw him again. He had on a red silk shirt and black pants. His shirt was partially unbuttoned and his pecs looked gorgeous. "Girl is that him?" "Yes it is." she said without taking her eyes off of him. "Now I can exhale." They laughed. Her pulse was racing and her temperature was rising. Red was fine. "Girl that brother is tight. Girl leave him to me and you call Jeronn." Trace looked at Teresa with a 'girl please' look.

"Teresa.. You're married." "Girl, please. The way that brother looks, I'd creep."

Trace and Red began to make some serious eye contact. It felt as if they were the only two people in the room. The music was hot and the atmosphere was sexy. Trace smiled as Red approached her. His stride was slow like sweet fudge. Shooo. He didn't *have* to be in a hurry. "Well, well, well." His voice oozed. "Red? It's nice to see you. This is my friend Teresa. Teresa this is Red." Red turned to Teresa momentarily without taking his eyes from Trace. "Nice to meet you Teresa." "Likewise Red." she put out her hand. He barely touched it and continued his eye dance with Trace. "Trace. You look exceptionally beautiful tonight. It's nice to see you. Is uh Jeronn joining you tonight?" "No. Just a night out with my girl" she smiled. She was almost blushing. "Mm dig that." He bit his bottom lip.

"So what are you ladies into tonight?"

"Actually we're not staying much longer." Trace felt herself wanting to giggle. She definitely had too much champagne. "Oh you're leaving? Well that's too bad. May I escort you ladies home?" He never took his eyes from Trace.

"Actually, Trace is staying at my house tonight." Teresa interjected. Déjà vu. "Is that so? Well Trace I really wouldn't mind seeing you home tonight." "Well actually," she cut Teresa off.

"Teresa I can speak for myself. I really was going to stay with Teresa tonight, but thanks for the offer. Will you excuse us? Teresa could you join me in the ladies room?"

"Excuse us Red bone. Oops, I mean Red." Teresa laughed. Red licked his lips and returned to his party. In the bathroom Trace put a cold towel on her face and freshened her make up. "Teresa, I'm going home with him tonight." The statement was a matter of fact. "Trace girl are you crazy? You don't know that man."

"Girl. I have to. I can't help myself. I don't know why, but I just have to." "Girl I ain't mad at you. His eyes so green you can see right through'em. And girl is it me or does he look like Terrence Howard?" "OOH I was thinking the same thing." They laughed. "Girl that man makes you wants to be nasty."

"Well I told you what he did to me that night me and Jeronn spent the night at his house." "Girl I wish it was me. So are you going to shuttle back with him or what?" "Hey I see no reason why we can't all shuttle back together."

"Cool." They snapped their fingers and laughed. When they exited the bathroom Trace was more nervous than before. How was she going to get Red to extend his invitation again tonight without sounding like a loose goose. They made their way over to his booth. She smiled elegantly. "So Red, how about shuttling us back to the main land?" Red put down his napkin and eased out of the booth. He turned to his friends and asked them if they would like a ride back to the shore on his boat. They told him they'd pass and get a shuttle later. The women seemed a little miffed that he was leaving, but what could they say? Red was the man. He opened his arms for both ladies to hold and escorted them outside. Back on the shore Red asked Trace if she would like to have a nightcap.

"You don't waste any time do you?"

"You get more done that way." He talks so smooth her panties were about to walk off her body on their own.

"Trace my car is right over here. Why don't you just call me in the morning?" Teresa informed more than asked. "Are you sure? I mean are you safe to drive?"

"Girl I'm fine. Trust me if anything happens I'll be calling Reggie to pick me up. Don't worry about me. Have a good time tonight and be safe."

"I will. I'll call you tomorrow." They hugged. Red never took his eyes off of her. She felt his stare. Her nipples were getting hard.

"Well Red. Looks like that nightcap is sounding better and better."

"Great baby. Your chariot awaits." He opened the door to his limousine and climbed in behind her. The leather seats were cozy. He turned on some music and poured her a glass of wine. "So, Miss Reese. Where would you like to go?" She smiled. "What do you mean?" "Well I'm sure you want to go some place where you won't be noticed. I mean, I noticed everyone checking you out tonight in the V.I.P. room and I said to myself, she must get tired of going places and not being able to enjoy herself. People wanting autographs and just to be around you."

"Hey it comes with the territory." she smiled. "You get used to it."

"Good. That's great. So then you won't mind signing me an autograph tonight?" She gave him a big smile. "Of course not." She sat her drink down. "Gimme a pen and paper." "Naw baby. I want you sign right here." He opened his shirt and exposed his stomach. *It should be a sin for a man to have a stomach like that* she thought. She exhaled.

"You work out a lot I see." "I try." he smiled. She licked her lips. "Listen, since you said you don't play games, I should be up front with you." She lowered her voice and spoke directly in his ear. "You and I both know what's going to happen tonight. You and I both know that it's gonna be good. But what I want you to know is that, I love Jeronn. Tonight doesn't take away from that. Are we clear?"

"Sweet heart. Jeronn who?"

"Alright. Just as long as you know." "Baby Jeronn ain't got nothing to do with what Dirty Red does. Dirty Red handles his business. You know what I'm saying?"

"Alright Dirty Red. Just making things clear."

"So now. Where to?"

"You know what. I have a nice little place just outside the city that we can go to. Is that alright with you?"

"Baby that's cool. Whatever you want. Private place huh? I like your style." After they arrived at her place, Trace noticed she had three messages on her machine. She didn't bother to check them. She was actually glad Red was here tonight. Just in case that creepy man showed up again outside her door. She knew Jeronn wouldn't dare show his face here again after last night. No matter though, she put better locks on the door. There was no way he was going to be able to break into that. She grabbed a bottle of wine from the refrigerator and showed Red to her room. "Why don't you make yourself comfortable while I go change." She went into the bathroom and changed into some sexy white lingerie and a smile. *You look good girl* she told herself in the mirror. She freshened her perfume and checked her body and prepared for passion. When she returned, Red had lit some candles and poured the wine. The music was soft and he looked good. He lay on the bed waiting for her. There was no more time for talk. At first they made love like animals. Trying to satisfy

something deeper than the flesh. Trace hadn't felt this good in a long time.

Not even the night that she and Jeronn made love in Red's own house.

Red was freaky. He did things to her body that she hadn't felt in years. He

was stroking her the whole time they made love. He kissed her throughout

their whole love making session. He barely took his lips off of her. His

fingers massaged every space and orifice on her body. After they made

love for the fourth time Red fell asleep. Trace couldn't sleep. She had

been here before. After one of her male friends would screw her for an

hour or even for ten minutes he would lay there exhausted and ready for

sleep. She couldn't sleep because she didn't love the men. She didn't want

them holding her and she really wanted them out of her bed. She just

enjoyed their company and thought how sad and idiotic they were for not

knowing who she really was. But tonight was different. Her reason for

not being able to sleep was different this time. Tonight she couldn't sleep

because she couldn't stop thinking about Jeronn. He was on her mind.

Red satisfied every part of her body. She couldn't deny that. But her

mind was still reeling from the events of dawn. She wondered if one of

the messages on the machine were from him. But then again, he didn't

have the phone number to this place. She had turned her cell phone off

before she even went to the club. She knew she would probably have a couple of messages on there. She went into the bathroom to wash up. She turned the water on and brushed her teeth. She stood there for a long time thinking about Jeronn and his problem. Should she help him or what? Can she forget what he did to her? It seems ironic that after he dumped her and left her to take care of everything by herself, her career and Chanelle that now he's in deep and he wanted her help. She used to pray for the day she could get back at him for leaving her the way he did. For cheating on her and breaking her heart. She used to wish for the opportunity for him to fail so that she could do to him what he did to her and rub it in his face. But she still loved him. She loved everything about him. She thought about Red laying in her bed. *He was good*, she smiled to herself. That man had all the right moves. Her body throbbed when she thought about what they had just done. It was that ache you get when you know you've just been laid well. She wanted to hurry up and climb back in bed with him. He made her feel good and nasty and she liked it. It was like a movie and she loved playing the role. When she had finished in the bathroom she clicked off the light and stepped into the room. What she saw nearly caused her a heart attack. She opened her mouth to scream but nothing came out. She wanted to panic, but her legs wouldn't move. She stood there shocked at what she saw.

Chapter Seventeen

Jeronn hadn't seen Trace in over twenty-four hours. He had been calling the house but Maja said she wasn't there. He knew Maja wouldn't lie. He was even forced to call Ross Langley, which he dreaded doing but he was getting desperate. He was tempted to go back to her apartment, but he didn't have the nerve. For all he knew she'd already filed a police report. He couldn't believe how stupid he had been. When he saw her laying in that bed next to that dude he just lost track of his senses. He wanted to hurt her. He wanted to hurt her the way he was hurting. He'd been trying to reach her all day but she wouldn't answer her cell phone. He figured she wouldn't come back here after what happened last night. He thought, she could be at a hotel or something. What Trace must think of him was eating him up inside. Ross Langley was only too happy to share that he couldn't find Trace either, but he was glad that Jeronn couldn't find her. The day she walked out of the house he thought she'd be gone for a little while as she calmed down, but he had no idea she would go and sleep with another man, let alone turn a trick with another man. When he saw her laying there wearing that wig, he knew what she was up to. He had thought she wanted to put that life behind her.

Maybe she's with one of her friends, he thought. He would just wait it out and let her contact him. He thought he'd hook up with his friend Red tonight, but changed his mind because he knew if he hooked up with him, he'd for sure be doing coke. So he decided to just go to his favorite hang out and have a couple of drinks and go home. He hadn't been in the studio in awhile. After his movie calamity he didn't have much of a drive to work on his music.

After he had a few drinks at the club he went home and sat in his studio. He looked around at all the unfinished business he had to take care of. He had several messages on his machine, but none from Trace. He had one message from his a friend telling him about a new group he wanted him to take a look at. He said they were hot and he let them sing a little acapella on his answering machine. They were good. He decided to give them a call in the morning. In the meantime he kept himself busy by working on his music and thinking about what he would say to Trace when she finally did call.

Jeronn woke up around 6:30 a.m. He felt like something wasn't right and he was upset that he hadn't heard from Trace yet. He tried her cell phone again, but there was still no answer and her voice mail was full so he couldn't leave her a message. He dressed to go for a run and clear his head. He had no idea what he was going to do about Trace and the situation they were now in. He certainly didn't think telling her his problem would cause her to do something like this. He knew she had a dinner engagement tomorrow night and he intended to be there to see her. Ross Langley had at least given him that much information. Jeronn no more liked Ross than Ross liked him, but they were both concerned about Trace and that at least made them equal. Jeronn felt satisfied in being able to tell Ross that he had already told Trace about his past and that he would not be getting the pleasure of telling her for himself. He didn't however tell him that it was that information that caused Trace to disappear. He was beginning to get a headache from thinking about Trace and what she must be going through. He wanted her to know that he wasn't the same man that he was all those years ago. He wanted her to trust him. But how could she after what he'd tried to do to her yesterday? He thought how selfish he's been to have treated her the way he had in the past and now here he was needing her help. Needing her to help get his career back on track. How could he have taken advantage of her like that? He vowed to himself, that if he were ever given a second chance with Trace he wouldn't screw it up.

Jeronn called his friend about the group he had heard on his answering machine and set up a time for them to come to the studio. He didn't have the money to commit to giving them a set contract, but he knew how to get them to the right place. He hated himself for the situation he was in, but he knew he had to get himself back out there to get the ball rolling. Just as he was about to try and call Trace again, his phone rang. He prayed it was Trace. It wasn't. It was Retha.

"So I guess you and your woman didn't work out huh?" "What are you talking about Retha? And why are you calling me?" Retha was the last person he expected to hear from.

"Oh yeah. You and your woman ain't working out like you thought you would huh? Getting your pictures all in the papers. But thang's not working out for ya huh Jeronn?"

"Is this going some place or am I hanging up this phone?"

"Oooh. I guess you don't know. The crap hasn't dripped its way down to your neck of the woods yet huh? Well let me hook you up with the latest since you obviously don't read the paper." He was getting annoyed with her voice.

"Well if you would open the newspaper you would see a picture of your current woman on the arm of player-player Dirty Red. Mm Hmm!! Aw yeah. Miss Reese was seen leaving the V.I.P. at the Miranda with Da Man himself last night. And if you think the story is not true. Let me let you hear it from the horses' mouth. I was there." Jeronn's heart felt like it had stopped. Panic was setting in. But he couldn't hang up on her. He had to listen.

"Girlfriend had on a little red dress and was all over ya boy last night. Her and her girlfriend. They probably had a ménage' a trios. I knew she was a tramp. But don't feel bad Jeronn. I'm sure it was nothing. Just run on out and get yourself a copy of the Herald. It's in the entertainment section. I'm sure they have whatever facts I can't fill in." Jeronn was quiet. He couldn't say a word. He had to appear like her words didn't bother him. But they did. And for Retha of all people to be the one to tell him that Red and Trace were together last night. It tore him up inside. What was he to do? "Well Jeronn. Your silence is golden. Just thought I'd call and give you some gossip. It's the least I could do being your ex-wife and all. You still broke Jeronn?"

"Good bye Retha." "Good bye?? I just told you about the freak of the week and that's all you can say to me? You should've tried to keep things tight with me Jeronn. You wouldn't be going through this right now." She started laughing. Mocking him.

"You ever heard that song *it's cheaper to keep her* Jeronn? Well that's what I should be singing to you. You should've tried to keep me cause I'm

195

going to run your ass through the ringer." She was laughing hard now.

"Well. I guess I'll go now. Just wanted you to hear the news from the

horses mouth in case you didn't believe your own eyes in the paper."

"You're right Retha. You are a horse." He hung up. That felt good. He

got the last word and it made him feel better. Momentarily. When he

thought about what Red and Trace were doing together it made him sick.

How could she do this to him? She wasn't somewhere suffering at all.

She's out kicking it with his boy, like it didn't mean a thing. He loved her

and he was trying to be honest with her and have a loving relationship with

her and she repays him like this? Did he mean nothing to her? He felt

stupid. How could he be feeling this way? It's the exact thing he had done

to her. He had no right. He thought that after last night she would be

feeling as bad as he did, but she seemed to have moved right along. His

mind called her every whorish name in the book; his heart prayed that it

wasn't true.   And there was no way he could confront Red. Red was not

the type of man you could show your weakness to. The bad part was, it

was in all the papers. He needed a drink. He had nothing left in the house.

He went to the market to buy a paper and a pint of Peppermint Schnapps.

He had been calling Trace's cellular phone the minute after he hung up on

Retha. She wasn't answering at home and he knew Chanelle must have

read the papers too. Chanelle had talked to her mom, but she didn't know

196

where she was. She told Jeronn not to worry. He could tell she had no clue who Red was, but he knew. He didn't tell her. He realized that he didn't actually know the number to her private apartment, but there's no way she would be there. Not with Red anyway. He started dialing Red's number non-stop. He called his cellular phone. He called his phone in his car and he couldn't reach him. For all he knew Red took her out on his boat or flew her out of town somewhere. That was his style. Jeronn was beginning to feel depressed. He was desperate and he hadn't felt this way in a long time. His friend came over later in the afternoon with the group Jeronn was interested in. He couldn't see him. He never even answered the door. His friend left a note under the door, but he just couldn't move. As the day turned into night, Retha had called to harass him a couple more times on the answering machine, but he couldn't answer. He didn't want to talk to her or anybody. Just Trace. How could she be this way? She was so cold. He thought of where he had found her that day. He thought he should expose her. He thought about how that would ruin her. But he couldn't do it. He wouldn't do that to her again. He was sloppy drunk by the time he realized someone was ringing the doorbell incessantly. He could barely see. His vision was blurry. He began yelling for an invisible dog to go and sic whomever was at the door. He got up and stumbled to the door carrying his vodka. He flung the door open. In his drunken haze he had a hard time making out the figure standing before him. For a moment, he thought it had to be Trace. He smiled. He reached out his hands for her. They felt heavy. "Baaabeee." He slurred. "Where have you been?"

"What took you so long to answer the door? It's starting to rain out here." He put his hands over his eyebrows as if it was bright and sunny instead of black as night outside. He couldn't see who was standing there. He recognized the voice. His face turned sour.

"What in the hell are you doing here?"

"Jeronn. I was worried about you. You didn't answer the phone and I realized what this must be doing to you." "Retha. Get the hell away from my door." He could barely get the words out. He could no longer stand up so he leaned against the coat rack and almost fell over. He put the hand with the bottle on his hip and stared at the floor. He felt bad. "Baby. I know what you're going through. Listen, I got something that'll make this all better."

"Retha. Go away." He sobbed. "I can't be bothered with you right now." He turned to walk away without closing the door. Retha let herself in. She went into the kitchen to put on a pot of coffee. Jeronn had no clue what was going on. He didn't want to know. Retha went upstairs into his bedroom to put on something dry and comfortable. His big T-shirt would do. She went into the kitchen and brought the coffee in to Jeronn. He yelled at her and tried to throw his bottle across the room at her. "Get the hell out of here. Why do you have on my clothes? You can't move back in Retha."

"Jeronn. Don't nobody want to move back in here with you. I just knew you were feeling bad. And I had to get out of those wet clothes so get off of my back."

"You have no idea what's going on here so you can just go back to wherever in the hell you came from." His words cut her. But what did she care? She couldn't stand Jeronn. But more than not liking Jeronn, she hated Trace. She hated Trace for all the years that she and Jeronn were together he compared her to Trace. Nothing she ever did was right. But she didn't care. She figured Trace had to come out in public sooner or later and when she did, she would see that Jeronn was just the same old bastard he always was. And what a pleasure it would be to see the look on Trace's face when she saw her walking around in Jeronn's clothes. She put a well-placed bug in someone's ear before her trek over here. She knew by tomorrow, one photographer or another would be snooping around on some gossip. She couldn't wait. She first needed to sober Jeronn up a bit. It wasn't going to be easy. She's seen him in this state before. "Jeronn, how about a nice massage to relax your body and your mind."

"I don't want you touching me. You can get out of here." She almost felt

sorry for him. She could tell he had been crying. His eyes were all puffy

and he was high as a kite. She looked in the ashtray and saw that he had

been smoking weed. Through some concerted effort, she got Jeronn into

the Jacuzzi, she massaged his back and rubbed his temples. She got a little

pleasure out of seducing him. His body was still the bomb. His muscles

were tight. And from the waste down, God had blessed him. She thought

it wouldn't hurt to get a little from him tonight. What's a little sex

between exes, she thought. Jeronn sobered up enough to realize he was in

his bathtub with a naked woman and that's all that mattered to him. He

pulled Retha in front of him and rubbed her hips. She smiled in his eyes

and let him have his way with her. She couldn't stand him any more, but

the sex was on. He squeezed her breasts too hard, but she didn't dare snap

him out of whatever daze he was in. He got out of the tub and picked her

up and took her into his room. It was almost mechanical. He never

looked at her. He never said a word. He laid her on the bed and made

love to her body. He licked her from head to toe but she could tell she

wasn't on his mind. Her wet body shivered in the coolness of the room.

His balcony doors were open. The rain was beating down hard outside.

He didn't notice. He buried his face between her brown thighs and

massaged her feet at the same time. He wasn't loving it. It wasn't like before. He was just doing it to be doing it and she could tell. She didn't say a word. She just lay back and enjoyed it. He pulled her to the edge of the bed and stood up. He brought her legs around his waist and picked her up. He had sex with her standing up. His face was remote. He lifted her body up and down into him. She loved it. He put her down on the bed and turned her around. He pulled her to him and rammed his body inside of hers. His breaths were fast and hard. She knew it was almost over. She half turned to look at his face and for a brief moment he looked at hers. He closed his eyes and collapsed on top of her. She lay on her stomach taking in his weight. She felt his sperm seep out of her onto the side of her thigh and down to the sheets. She felt empty. She felt like she had so many times before, when she wondered if he were thinking about Trace when they made love. She hated him for making her feel this way. But that was why she was here. Revenge. Tonight, she would make sure that the world thought that she and Jeronn were back together. She had no idea what he was thinking, but she knew for sure it wasn't about her and what they had just done. He never did. She eased from under Jeronn and he just climbed in the bed and went to sleep. She went into the bathroom and stared in the mirror. She hated this house. She hated the memories. She wondered if Trace and Jeronn had made love in that bed yet. She looked around the linen closet and in the medicine cabinet to see if there were any signs of a woman being there. There was nothing. Women who think they're slick always try and leave tampon boxes or a lipstick or something around like that's supposed to let another woman think that she's all apart of the mans life. When will women realize that if another woman is there to see that in the first place, you spot must not be as tight as you think? Duh! She thought to herself about how many times she'd done that. She'd leave a tampon box on the back of some man's linen shelf. Or her lipstick. Or an unused condom strategically placed for some other woman to find. She thought to herself how Trace was probably too uppity for something like that. That's okay. She'd get her uppity ass right where it hurt. When the papers get a wind of her and Jeronn tomorrow, it would be enough to make Trace's head swim. She remembered how jealous she felt when she read in all the papers that Miss High Society was back on the arms of her lost love Jeronn. It still rang badly in her ears. And it embarrassed the hell out of her. She couldn't go anywhere without someone realizing who she was and what was going on. And the fact that Jeronn practically ruined her career didn't help one bit. Yeah, she was going to get Trace back if it was the last thing she ever did on earth. And if Jeronn got hurt in the process so be it. Screw him. She didn't even wash up. She grabbed her purse and took out her little package. She pulled out a razor and made herself a line. She rolled up a bill and inhaled what she called 'her medicine'. She sat down on the bed and smiled. She turned to look at Jeronn's butt. It was tight. She thought about sticking something in it while he slept and laughed her head off. She was in no mood for sleeping so she sat there thinking what else she could do to get Jeronn and Trace back. She'd have to be satisfied for now with her plan. She knew that Trace was going to be at the Moxy tomorrow night for a closed birthday performance for the President of her record company and she figured Trace and Jeronn were supposed to be going together.

Chapter Eighteen

Trace moved slowly toward her bureau to reach for her gun. She didn't know if it was loaded, but she had to get it anyway. Here she was standing here stark naked in front of Red and some strange fool holding a gun on Red. She panicked. Red spoke first.

"Hold on now. Don't get excited. Let's just give the man what he wants and everybody is cool." Graham stood there feeling full of himself. He had caught her in the act. He didn't want to hurt her for sure, but his payday was here. She was up in this apartment with her john still naked on the bed.

"Now listen Miss Reese. I know who you are and I know what you're doing up here." Trace squinted her eyes. There was something familiar about him. "What do you want? Just take it and go." She spoke calmly.

"Oh it's not that easy. I was just standing here thinking to myself. I didn't know you had all this beauty going for you. So maybe, I'll just tie up your friend here and see what else I might want to help myself to. If you don't mind."

"Nigga what in the hell are you talking about?" Red started moving. "Oh don't play dumb with me. You had your turn. But I suppose you're going to sit there and tell me that you didn't know you were sleeping with a prostitute. But what I can't understand is how come you don't recognize her." Trace figured out who he was. He was the fool standing at her door the day Jeronn found her there. He had come back. He was about to tell all her business to the last person she would ever want to know.

"You are crazy mister and I have no idea what you're talking about. I think you've got the wrong person."

"Oh I think I have the right person. Those bullets you sweatin' tells me I know for sure I got the right person."

"Listen man. This woman is not a prostitute. This is Trace Reese. The singer? Now you know she's got money. She can get you whatever you need. So why don't you put down that gun and let's just talk about this okay? Hell, I got money. I will give you whatever you need brotha. It's no problem." Red was working his magic. Graham momentarily looked at Red and thought he recognized him too, but he couldn't place the face.

"Go head. Look over there in them pants over there. I'm sure you're going to find just what you want right there." Graham moved slowly over to the pants. He patted them and felt the pockets. Inside he felt a small brown vile filled with cocaine. He threw it on the floor. "Drugs!" he was indignant.

"You think I came up here because I want drugs? Oh no no no. I don't have a drug problem. I have a money problem. And let me just get down to business here. Either you give me one million dollars or I'm going to tell the whole world about your little sexual escapades that you participate in up in this apartment." Trace swallowed hard. She had no idea how long this man had known about her. She decided to keep her mouth shut and hopefully Red would think the guy was just crazy. But Red picked up on some familiarity here. The man turned down drugs so he knew he couldn't be all that crazy.

"Look here man. Tell me what you need. Red's got it for ya."

"Okay. Red!" He spoke indignantly. He started waving the gun. "I want one million dollars or I tell the whole world here that Trace Reese is a prostitute."

"Prostitute? Man why do you keep saying that? The lady and I are friends. Very good friends. Do I look like I need to pay for some pussy?" He didn't want to make Trace feel cheap. But what did he care. This fool had a gun on him.

"Brother. Surely you know who Dirty Red is. I don't need to pay for pussy from no hoe.' But like I said. Miss Reese and I are very good friends. I think you have the wrong person. Besides, if she were a prostitute don't you think the whole world would know about it by now?" Graham began to smile.

"Oh but they will. They definitely will if she doesn't come up with one million dollars by tomorrow. I'm going to tell the world that she sleeps with men for money."

"They wont believe you. If you just asked her for a million dollars, why would they believe a maniacal story like that? Now tell me what it is you really need and stop waving that damn gun around." Trace was quiet. She couldn't speak. This man knew the truth. She couldn't let him expose her this way. She couldn't let him do it. She was speechless. She had come too far to be exposed this way. She knew if she made any sudden moves that he might shoot her and Red too. She couldn't be responsible for that. She started sweating more. The music on the radio was turned down. She thought maybe she could scream, but then she knew for sure he'd shoot them. She couldn't get to her gun. She pointed to the dresser when Graham wasn't looking. Red got the picture.

"Look man. I don't know what you think is up. But I know that this woman sleeps with men for money. Whether she's famous or not. Check her answering machine. I'm sure there's something on there that will tell you. I know what she's all about. I don't know how she keeps men from finding her out, but she does. You're good lady. And I can see why the men love you so much." She quickly grabbed a pillow from the floor and covered her body as much as she could. Red turned to look at her and signaled he had no way of getting to that dresser with Graham standing there in front of it.

"Look man. What's your name? We can work something out here. There's no need to go out like this."

"Oh I ain't going out at all. You may not be one of her johns but she definitely is a whore. Go ahead. Check the answering machine. I'll let you do the honors." Tears began to roll down Trace's face. Her worst nightmare had come true. Someone had found out her shameful secret. It was like a bad movie. She had no idea what those messages on that machine were. They could be dull and uninformative in which case her secret would still be hidden from Red. Or they could be explicit and to the point in which case she felt like a complete fool. "Please don't," she whispered. The tears were hot and heavy now. Red and Graham both stopped in the middle of the room. Graham began to smile. He could feel his payday already. "Trace. What's up?" Red asked.

"Just please don't touch the answering machine." She swallowed hard. "Okay, okay. Don't get upset." Red was a cold-blooded man, but he didn't want to do anything to intentionally break her down like that. There was something about her. "Alright. It's cool. No need. Look man, like I said. Money is not a problem. Why don't you just let me use my phone and I can get you the money you need in an hour. You can be on your way and this never has to go any further."

"Oh just like that huh? Well you certainly are captain save a hoe ain't you? Well since it's that easy and you seem to be the one doing all the talking how bout two million?"

"Alright. Two million, but then you have to leave and never come back here. Ever again" "You assuming that I'm going to let you live after this man. You see, you're not even the person I came to see and our ungracious hostess here isn't saying a damn thing. So what do you have to say for yourself Miss Reese? How come you ain't saying nothin' over there? Let me answer that. Because you're boyfriend was almost about to find out our little secret wasn't he?"

"I can get you the money in the morning." She replied.

"Fine. I ain't going anywhere."

"Can I get dressed?" she asked.

"Of course. I don't want you to feel uncomfortable in your own home. But then again, you're probably comfortable with your clothes off." Graham laughed. He hadn't counted on coming in on her and a date. He just thought he'd surprise her. He came to the door and heard music. He thought she might be sleep at this time of morning. Trace moved over to the dresser and pulled a shirt out of the middle drawer. She slipped it on. She pulled open her underwear drawer and searched for her gun.

"If you're looking for your gun it's gone. Just put your panties on and back away from the dresser miss sweet thing." She gritted her teeth. She felt like a fool. Red was standing with his pants on and shirt off. He even looked good with a gun pointed at him.

"So how about it man. I can get you the money you want here in a couple of hours. All you have to do is say the word and be outta here."

"Well, Miss Reese. I'm game. What do you think of that?" Graham was feeling very powerful calling all the shots. He knew he still had her secret. Even if he took the money and ran she knew, he knew. His only proof was a couple of notes he had stolen from under her door when he had visited a few times waiting for her to return. It had taken almost three months, but he knew she'd be back.

"I said I'd pay in the morning."

"Trace. Baby I can get you out of this in five minutes. Just let me make a phone call." Red was trying to reason with Trace and the man with the gun. He knew under any other circumstances he would have whacked this fool by now, but he was disarmed the minute the man walked in the room.

"You don't understand." She flopped on the bed.

"What's to understand? You need to get this man off your back and I can do it for you. Besides, I like living. So let's just give him what he wants and move on." She turned to Red. She thought she may as well tell him what Graham was talking about. Sooner or later he was going to start believing it anyway. She had already freaked out about the answering machine. She got up her courage and she began pacing the room. She looked at Graham sternly in the face and all of a sudden she didn't care. She needed to say it out loud. She went over to her lamp desk and pulled out her weed. She lit a joint. She sat on her chaise and began telling Red her story. Red just sat and listened. She walked out of the room when she was finished. She sat on the sofa and waited for the men to come into the room. She knew they would. The gunman wouldn't let her sit in there alone not knowing what she was doing. Red came out first followed by Graham pointing the gun at him. When Red sat down on the leather sofa across from her, she hit the button on the answering machine. She didn't know what was on it, but she had an idea. The first one was from a guy in the governor's office.

Baby. I miss your loving. I've been so bad. I need a spanking. You don't know how much I miss you. Call me. That didn't really tell a story so she waited. There were two more. The second message was Den. She immediately recognized the voice and knew what it was going to say.

I don't know what that was all about last night, with your boyfriend catching us in the bed like that. If you're free tonight, gimme a call.

Trace was so embarrassed. She put her head down and looked at Red. But, what the hell? May as well get it all out there. She had told him most of the story anyway. The last message was Dennis again. And it was the tell all of her double life. *Hey Miriam. If you don't answer the phone when I call, I'm going to be forced to take my business elsewhere. And from what I remember, you love my business.* He hung up. So her secret was out there. She turned to Graham.

"Now you bastard. Two of you know about the secret. Now what? Huh? What if he beats you to the telling? You wont have a fucking leg to stand on. So go ahead. Shoot me. I don't give a fuck." She got up and went to the bathroom and slammed the door. She slid down to the floor and sobbed. She sobbed hard. She didn't come out of the bathroom for a long time. After almost an hour, she opened the door and watched as Red handed Graham over a black duffle bag and a rather large Chinese man stood at her front door. She didn't move. She saw Red hand the gunman his card and tell him, if you want to stay rich, give him a call. Graham left the apartment. The Chinese man left the apartment. Red turned to the bathroom door where he saw Trace cowering through the crack. "You can come out now." She opened the door wider. Her eyes were burning and she felt sick in the light of day.

"Why did you give that man money and let him walk out of here like that?"

"Listen. That man is just an average fool like the rest of them out there. "

"You paid that motherfucker to keep a secret that wasn't yours? Do you actually think he's going to walk the hell out of here and never tell what he knows? What makes you think he wont come back and extort money from me or worse yet, kill my black ass?"

"Trace. Calm down okay. I've been talking to that man. You don't have anything to worry about from that brother. And yes I paid him to keep your secret. But I also paid him to work for me. You wont ever have to worry about him again. Besides, I got somebody taking care of him as we speak?"

"That big Chinese man that was standing here?"

"No. That big Chinese man is keeping an eye on me. I have some one else assigned to him." "Red," She threw her hands in the air. "You must think I'm some kind of damned fool."

"No. I don't think anything like that. After listening to you last night and listening to Graham this morning. That's the gunman's' name by the way. It's Graham Watkins. Anyway, I'll tell you, even Dirty Red needs his dose of reality every now and then."

There was a knock at the door. Trace became panicked again. "Don't worry. I had someone bring us some breakfast. I figured we could both use it. I usually like to dine in my silk robe, but I think this will be suitable what do you think." He was laughing. He was trying to get a smile out of her. It was barely working. After eating, he asked Trace if she was going to give Jeronn a call and tell him about her ordeal.

"No." She chewed her strawberry. "So you're not ever going to tell him your secret?" "Jeronn knows." Red was shocked. "Whaaaat? Well well well. Jeronn knows. So I take it that you haven't been shall we say..indulging since you and Jeronn got back together?"

"That's right. No need to." She threw her strawberry down.

"This doesn't make sense to me. A man holds a gun on you all night. He threatens to end your life and mine. He tells you my dirty secret. And you and him are buddies now?"

"Oh no. I never said that. I said he would never bother you again. And as far as your secret goes..." He knelt down in front of her. His beautiful green eyes piercing her heart strings. They were full of sincerity.

"You never, ever have to worry about me doing anything to make you look bad. There's something about you Trace that makes me want to do right. I can't explain it and I know you're with Jeronn, but girl you got something that most of these knuckleheaded women out there will never have. Black, White, Red, Asian, Indian, I don't care. You got something. Unfortunately, Red can't be tied down like that." He smiled and stood up.

His pedicured feet slapping across her hard wood floor. He went into the bedroom to shower. Trace crept over to the door and peeked through the keyhole. She didn't yet feel secure. She saw the big Chinese man standing outside her door. That was one big bodyguard. She went over to the window and saw Red's limo sitting outside with another man standing by it. She had to get him out of here before he drew attention. She was definitely getting rid of this apartment. Today. She heard the shower running and became curious. She crept over to Red's pants to pull out his wallet. Just as she was about to open it he was behind her. "It's Anthony. Anthony Jones." She froze. She turned around and smiled as he stood there glistening in all his sexy maleness. He glided over to her. "How did you know what I was doing?"

"Baby. I know women. Women are all basically the same. Curious."

"I thought you just said I was different?" She smiled. "You are. But you're still a woman," he paused. "So, I take it you won't be staying here much longer?"

"You take it right."

"And I suppose the world will never know that you even had this place. Is that right?" "Right again," she smiled.

"Well, since this is your last day in this place, allow me to do the honors of helping you say good bye?"

"How?" she smiled again. He took her to the bed and laid her down. He pulled her shirt over her head and caressed her body. Her nipples were getting extra hard. He rubbed her stomach and it made her self-conscious. She still didn't like that fact that she had stretch marks and couldn't get rid of them. Red climbed over her and planted soft kisses on her forehead, neck and shoulders. He kissed her hot and gently. She felt her body becoming warm. He pulled her head up by the hair and pulled her face to his. He stared into her eyes. He wanted to comfort her hurt soul. He wanted this time spent to wipe away all the bad she felt. He knew he couldn't change her life or her past, but he could certainly help her to realize it didn't matter. He kissed her all over. He tasted every inch of her. Her body was on fire. He put his fingers between her legs and gently pressed them inside of her. She inhaled. He took his fingers out of her and rubbed his hand across her lips. She looked in his eyes. He kissed her lips. He tasted her. He wanted her. He turned her to the side and lay behind her. They faced the window as he lifted her leg and went inside her. He held her leg in the air and loved her deeper. His cheek was against hers as he held her closer. She wanted to scream. He was wonderful. She tried to push Jeronn out of her mind, but his face kept creeping in.

After it was over they lay there for a while staring at the ceiling. Just

thinking. "When will this nightmare end? I need to ask you something?"

"What's that?" he asked. "While you were in the shower I started

wondering. First of all how did you get that creep to just walk away from

his path of destruction and two how can I be sure that something else like

this won't happen?"

"Well as far as that creep is concerned, he never wanted to hurt you. If he

did, he had the chance to kill me when you were in the bathroom last

night. He had his chance to get rid of me and handle his business with

you, which is what he came here to do in the first damn place. That man is

just another hustler who's too damned lazy to get a real job, but he wants

to be rich. I've seen many men like him. And just so you know, I didn't

give him two million dollars." He fixed himself a drink. He smiled and

swirled his orange juice. After crunching on his ice he said, "Ain't no way

in hell I was giving that nigga two million dollars. I gave him a big head

start. So that's how you know he won't be back to bother you. Besides

you're moving out of here right? No apartment, no story to tell." She put

her head down and stared out the window. She just wanted this

embarrassing nightmare to be over. She never in a million years wanted

Red to know what she had been doing.

"So what do you think of me?" she asked. "The same thing I thought when I first met you. You fine as hell girl? What you did in your past is your business. I thought I just finished proving that to you twenty minutes ago." They smiled at each other.

"Red after all this I'm just not ready to face the world." "Well why don't I just cancel a few appointments and stay here with you until you're ready?" "That would be wonderful. But I have a plane to catch. I had a singing engagement tomorrow night. It's my boss's birthday. I'm just too tired. She sighed. "I had heard about that. Need an escort?"

"No. I think I'll just cancel and get a plane. He'll understand. Besides all my family is in Chicago, it'll do me some good to get out of here and visit them."

"When are you leaving for Chicago again?"

"Sometime today. I have to do Oprah in the morning. I need some rest. I was supposed to call Jeronn so he could go with me, but I don't feel like dealing with that right now. Plus we've got some things to work out. And don't worry, I wont tell Jeronn about all the wonderful things we did in this apartment."

"Baby I'm not worried. I'm a man. And I don't answer to any body."

"Red you are too much." Trace spent almost an hour on the phone with Ross Langely telling him to stop worrying about her and she would be in touch right after the Oprah show tomorrow morning. She told him to cancel her showing at the party tonight. Red had arranged for her to fly out of the airport on his chartered plane in 2 hours. He said he would pack up the apartment for her have everything cleaned out and moved to storage. He gave her a ride to the airport in his limo. She handed him the keys to her car. Red told her if she stayed in Chicago for a few days he would maybe come down there and they could chill out together. She told him the hotel she would be staying in and said she'd give him a call. She had never imagined him to be the caring type but he surprised her. She imagined him to always be on the go. He told her he *was* always on the go. He told her of his involvement in politics and his international conquests. But being the master of his domain, he called the shots. She had a lot of respect for Red. Even though he was rude to the bone, she liked him. Maybe in another time and another place she could have been his leading lady, but that wasn't the life for her. Her life involved, Christianity, Christ, love and marriage. Red wouldn't be going down that road for a long time and she knew that. He kissed her on the forehead and she boarded the plane. She waved good-bye to Red and leaned back in the chair thinking of Jeronn.

Chapter Nineteen

Jeronn woke up with a splitting headache. He was used to this when he

drank all night. He stumbled to his medicine cabinet and took two

Tylenol. Entering his room he realized that there was another body in his

bed. He hadn't paid attention when he got up because it was covered

under the sheet. He looked at the foot sticking out and realized he'd

recognize that ugly toe ring anywhere. His stomach turned as he tried to

remember the events of last night. He remembered Retha coming to the

door but he didn't remember anything else. She snored lightly. He

noticed on the dresser that she must have been partying because there were

still a couple of lines on the dresser. He tried to remember if he had taken

any. He figured she'd be sleep for a while so he hopped in the shower to

get dressed. The party was tonight and he and Trace had planned to go

together. He would stake himself out at her house all day until she

returned. There was no way she would miss this. He put the thought of

her having sex with Red out of his mind. She would never do that, he

thought. First he had to get rid of the banshee so he can get going. He

heard Retha stirring and hoped she'd get the hell out without so much as a

word. No such luck. She stood in the doorway behind him looking like a

hot nappy-headed mess. Her hair was all over her head and she was wearing his basketball jersey. He hated her.

"I guess I'll be burning that jersey when you take it off. Unless you want to take it with you." She smiled. She had no harsh words for him. She knew her revenge was coming soon. "Jeronn. Why don't I fix you some breakfast? You had a really hard night last night and it's the least I could do."

"Look. I don't really know what went on here last night. But we're not back together and I still don't want to have anything to do with your evil ass." He pulled his towel tight around his waist. "You don't have to do that baby. I saw all I needed to see last night." "Oh really. Well keep it to yourself. I've conveniently blocked it out of my mind. Do you mind? I need to get dressed?"

"Oh sure baby. I don't mind. I'll just run down stairs and get breakfast started before I get ready and go." "Whatever." He rubbed himself down with lotion. Retha crept down stairs wearing nothing but a smile when she noticed a guy hiding in the bushes with a camera. She knew who it was and she knew what he was doing there. She had given a little tip to a friend whom she knew would pass it on to the right people. Jeronn may not be super hot in the show business world any more, but good gossip, was gossip nonetheless. She cracked the door open and said out loud to noone.." I'll just get the paper baby and I'll meet you in for breakfast." She opened the door wide and boldly walked out to get the paper. She bent down letting her breasts hang without trying to cover them. She turned slowly so the camera could get enough pictures. She wasn't ashamed of her body. She looked good. And her intentions were more important than what anybody thought of her body. She crept back in slowly. She gently closed the door and ran upstairs to get dressed. When Jeronn came down he was not happy to see that Retha was still there. "Don't you have another house you need to haunt?" "Whatever. I'm leaving. I just thought I'd be here for you in your time of despair."

"I'm not in despair Retha. I trust Trace. Regardless of what this paper says and regardless of what you say. Especially of what you say."

"Yeah right Negro. Is that why you looked like a limp puppy when I got here last night?"

"First of all, ain't nothing limp about anything on me. Second of all I didn't look like a limp puppy. You looked like a wet dog standing out there in the rain and I felt sorry for you.

So you pack up your hoochie bags and get the hell out of my house."

"That's Gucci."

"Whatever." He threw the paper down after scanning for anything about Trace. There was nothing mentioned except in the society column about the dinner for the evening. He escorted Retha out of the house and hopped into his car. She hopped in hers and pulled up along side of him. He wasn't leaving until he was sure she was gone. She let her window down and stared him deeply in the eyes. "Payback is a mother." After which she sped off. He yelled. "Yeah whatever," and drove off. He went to pick his tux up from the cleaners before heading his way over to Trace's.

The next morning at five a.m., Trace left to head over to the studio. She had to be at Oprah's at 6 a.m. The show was taped live and she needed to get ready. She wasn't really in the mood but it was her job and her life. She called Chanelle and told her that she had visited her Grandma last evening and told her everything that was going on with the family. She told her Jeronn had called a million times. They talked about her granddaughter and Trace headed for the studio. The studio had called three times to ask her what she required in her dressing room. She called Ross. She told Ross to handle everything. The only thing she wanted to think about was getting dressed. She thought about Red and gave him a call from the limo.

"Were you able to handle everything?"

"I told you I would."

"Well I appreciate it. Where did you park the car?"

"At your home. I had the keys given to your housekeeper. I had Mai to deliver them." Trace was annoyed at that but what could she do? "Well tell Mai I said thank you. Did you have to explain that to her at all?"

"I told you, I don't have to explain anything to anybody. So how is your trip so far?"

"It's fine. I saw my mom last night and the rest of my family. We're not that close but it's getting better."

"Well that's good to hear. So have you decided how long you would be staying there?"

"I don't know. I just need to get away for awhile."

"Well I could be down there sometime tonight if you like. Maybe hang out with you. Play some backgammon." She smiled. "Thanks Red. I'll let you know. Have you heard from Jeronn?"

"No, but I guess that means you haven't either."

"No I haven't. But I'll call him after the show. It's only 7 a.m. there and he thinks we're going to the party tonight.

"Maybe you should have told him ahead of time."

"There was never any time. It's only 6a.m. here so I'll call him in about an hour or so."

"Alright then."

"Well I'll give you a call when I get back to the hotel." "Bye."

She thought about him visiting her in Chicago and was almost tempted to make love to him one more time, but decided to let that go. Her time with Red in that apartment has been the best time she's ever spent in this place. It was time to close that chapter. You can't have too much of a good thing. She dressed at the studio and waited for hair and make up.

As they were fixing her up she sat there wondering was there anything that could make her soul pretty again? She was battered and bruised on the inside. She had put a lot of nonsense into her body, but how could she make that pretty again. She thanked God for all the blessings in her life. She was trying to hold back tears as they made up her face. She didn't want to tick them off by having them to do it again. But her heart became so filled that she couldn't hold back. She asked them to leave the room. When she was alone, she looked at herself in the mirror. She asked God to heal her. She asked God to forgive her for everything she had done since the day she left Him. She knew it was the Lord that had brought her safely to this day. Many times in that apartment she felt like there was another presence there. Like the Holy Spirit was telling her to just leave. But she couldn't. Her mind couldn't. Her body couldn't. Her flesh couldn't. She felt like she needed what she was getting. But today, of all days, she was filled with overwhelming emotion. She picked up the phone to call Jeronn. He wasn't there. She tried his cell phone. "Hi baby."

"Trace I am so sorry. I am so sorry for what I did. I am the worst person on the planet and I can never ever take back what I've done, but I ask you for your forgiveness right now. I am so sorry Trace."

"Jeronn you know what? It didn't happen. As far as I'm concerned, it didn't happen. I'm sorry as well. I'm in Chicago."

"What are you doing there? Is everything okay?"

"Well I'm doing the Oprah Show shortly and I wanted to visit my family."

"Well do you want me to come there?"

"Why don't you wait until I get back to the hotel and I'll return a call to you and let you know what I'm going to do?"

"Okay, if that's what you want. Are you sure you're okay?"

"Yeah I'm fine. Why?"

"Well, I don't know if this is the right time, but yesterdays' paper has a picture of you and Red all cozy up to each other. Saying you're an item and stuff. What's up with that?"

"Well you know Jeronn, I was out with Teresa and we ran into him. There's nothing much to tell you." "Are you sure?" he asked.

"Yeah. I'm sure." She felt honest about that answer.

"Okay then well I'll wait for your call."

"Alright then," They hung up. Jeronn wasn't satisfied with their conversation. But he realized that was going to have to wait. He felt like he was being followed. To be sure, he made a couple more turns and it turns out that he was. He drove to the police station and parked his car. He didn't know what was going to happen. As he pulled over, the black car slowed passed him and the window rolled down. "You running out of time Jeronn Clarke. You're number is coming up. If you don't want to be a statistic you better pay what you owe." And with that, they drove off. Jeronn knew exactly who had sent those goons. He went home and waited for Trace to call him. He was panicking. But he had to wait for her. He needed the money today. This was it for him. Trace had several messages when she returned to the hotel and she called her mom first. Her mom wanted her to come over for a barbecue and told her she was going to get a manicure and pedicure before she arrived. Her mom and brothers and sister were doing a lot better over the years. Once Trace's career took off, she took very good care of her family. She didn't mind. They were all doing well on their own, but anything she could do to help, she did. Ross called as soon as she hung up. He had his attitude on. Trace was not in the mood for it. He reamed her out about disappearing and not being able to be found. She had had enough of it. She had almost lost her life this past week and she was not about to be putting up with Ross' petty jealousy. "Listen Ross. I'm tired of you talking to me like I'm some little bitch you can command what to do and when to do it. There is nothing between us.

There never will be okay? Now just get that through your pretty little head before you're out on your ass and fired. I don't have time for this today okay?!" Ross was mute. In all the years he had known Trace she had never spoken to him this way. He would normally attribute this behavior to spending so much time with Jeronn, but he knew that Jeronn didn't have a clue as to where Trace had been either. "Trace. I'm sorry okay? I care a lot about you and I have for a long time." She put him on speakerphone and brushed her hair furiously. "I don't mean to upset you. I know you have a lot of things on your mind."

"Ross. I don't want to have to go off like this. I know you've been there for me through some really rough times. When Jeronn left me I didn't have a leg to stand on in this industry. You opened the right doors for me and put me in touch with all the right people. Whenever I accept an award, you're the first person I thank. Well the second. Gotta give praise to God Almighty." She smiled. "Ross what I'm saying is, I adore your friendship. I love who we are, but this is all we'll ever be. Okay?" "Yes. I understand. I know I over step my boundaries sometimes and I'm sorry. It's just that I care for you so much."

"I understand. Listen, I'll be back in a few days why don't we get together for lunch?"

"Sounds good to me." "Great. I'll talk to you then."

"I'm going to have a bath now and order some room service. I'll talk to you soon."

"You go and have a long bath. I'll take care of everything else." "Great, bye Ross. Oh Ross, Could you have my bracelet from Swarovski delivered to you? I was supposed to wear it and I called and put it on hold and so they never delivered it, but it's paid for. Just have it delivered or picked up if you don't mind?" "Sure Trace. Anything for you Miss Reese."

"Ross."

"I know I know. Just kidding." Trace settled into the tub and closed her eyes. The events of the last couple of days still swimming in her mind. She needed to give Jeronn a call soon. She desperately needed a massage, but she had no time for that now. She was glad for Chanelle and Ross. They saved her every time. She was so glad she didn't have to deal with packing that apartment. It was the last thing she ever wanted to do. She picked up the phone on the side of the wall and dialed Red's cell phone. He answered on the first ring.

"Miss me already baby?" She giggled. "Do you even know who this is?" "Of course I do. This that fine hot singer that can't get dirty enough." She blushed. "Anyway, I just wanted to call and thank you for taking care of the place for me. It's very considerate and you have been more than kind."

"So what you saying, there's some kind of reward in this for me?"

"No I didn't say that. I just wanted to thank you again for being there for me."

"Listen lady. You don't have a thing to worry about on this end. Okay? Now you just get yourself together and I'll see you tonight." "What do you mean?" she asked.

"I know you don't think the richest black man you've ever met would pass up a Friday night in the Windy City?"

"Oh my God are you coming to Chicago?"

"I'll be there in a couple of hours."

"Well to tell you the truth, I invited Jeronn to come and be with me."

"That's fine baby. I'm sure we'll get to see one another. Oh by the way, did he mention to you about the newspaper ad?"

"Yeah about seeing us in it. He told me. I just told him that we ran into each other that's all. No big deal."

"Well as long as everything is fine with you. I'll be in touch this evening lil' girl." She giggled. What was it about this man? He certainly heated her up. "Well just call me."

"Will do." He hung up. She called Theresa.

"Girl did you read the paper yesterday?"

"Girl yes! Can you believe they suggested a Ménage' a Trois?"

"Girl Reggie liked to lost his mind up in here, up in here." They cackled like hens.

"Girl I explained the whole thing to him and he totally understood. I told him that that was the night we took the boat out and he already knew that I came straight home to him so he was cool. So tell me what happened with you and Mr. Man." Trace told her they had spent two days together eating and drinking and being merry. She didn't tell her about the private apartment and what had happened. She wasn't ready to tell anyone that story yet. She told her that deep down he was such a gentleman. She told her his real name and they laughed some more. "What are you guys doing tonight?"

"Girl nothing. As she was leaning her head on the back of the tub she recognized a voice that could not be mistaken for anyone else. The high-pitched tones made the hairs on her back stand. She got out of the tub and grabbed a robe. She turned the television up. It was Retha. She was engaged in a conversation with some newswoman about being seen leaving Jeronn's home that morning. She was asking her if it meant they were back together. When she had talked to Jeronn earlier he said nothing about spending time with Retha. "Hold on Teresa. Have you seen the news? Is this on there?"

"What channel?"

"Whatever channel BET is there?"

"Hold on let me turn." Retha was going on and on about how they just wanted to spend some quiet time getting reacquainted. The newswomen in the room were all ears and tongues as Retha oozed out her juicy story about how Jeronn was still insatiable in the bedroom. Retha knew Trace would be watching this, she thought. Somehow she knew. Trace was pissed. Jeronn had been with Retha last night. The same woman he had left her for? She felt like she had no right to be upset considering what she had been doing with Red for the past two days, but it just wasn't the same. She was crushed and Jeronn was the wrecking ball. She hung up the phone. Teresa called back.

"It's probably not even true. She's always coming up with some piece of gossip or another. She's just like that you know?" Trace wished her words were true. But they probably weren't. She knew Jeronn probably felt bad after the way he had found her the other night. She felt she could forgive him for what he had done to her, but after this it was going to be hard. If it had been anybody else, she'd have been willing to put this behind. But it was Retha. The afternoon went by slowly.

When Jeronn finally showed up at her room he gave her the biggest kiss. She wanted to scratch the skin off of his face. Her mind wondered if he had made love with Retha the way they had made love at Red's house. She seemed distant and Jeronn could tell. He didn't know why, but he remembered that she said they would talk tonight. She put on her halter dress with slits up the sides and it was gorgeous. She looked stunning, but she didn't feel that way. She still had to go to her family's barbecue, no matter what. She freshened her make up and was leaving the room. Jeronn grabbed her and asked what was going on.

"What happened with Retha last night?" she demanded.

"What are you talking about?"

"I'm talking about you and Retha getting together last night. What happened?"

"I was drunk. I was upset about seeing you and Red together in the paper and she showed up at the door. After she came in I really don't remember much after that. I passed out. When I woke up this morning she was still there sleeping. I took a shower and got dressed. But baby I promise, I really don't remember much after that." She was hesitant to believe him.

"Well my family's having a barbecue, are you coming?"

"Just like that?"

"Just like that." She didn't have anything to say. She didn't want to be a hypocrite either. "While they were in her rented car Jeronn told her about the threat he received from the goons earlier that morning." He asked her for her help. He hated the situation they were both in, but he did

233

need her help. She told him she would help and everything would be fine. As they were driving, his cell phone rang. "Hello?"

"*Look out your rearview nigga!*" He jerked his head around. There was another car following him. "*Don't think just cause you leave town your problems go away. You got twenty four hours.*" They hung up.

"What's wrong Jeronn?" she asked.

"They're here. They followed me all the way here."

"Who the guys?"

"Yeah. They're actually following me."

"What?? I can't go to my family's house with someone following you like that."

"Go back to the hotel." She turned the corner and headed back. They hadn't seen the car after the phone call but they knew someone was following them. Trace rushed into her room. "What are we going to do?"

"Let me make a phone call." He went into the bedroom and made a call.

"She got on her cell phone to Red. She told him what was going on. He told her he would be there shortly. When Jeronn returned he told her what it would take to get them off their backs. She said she could handle that. She wanted to be sure that after they were paid off they wouldn't bother any of them ever again. A knock came to the door. When they opened it there was nothing there but a newspaper. On the front cover there was a picture of Retha stark naked standing on Jeronn's porch with blue circles covering her crotch area and breasts. She read the story and passed the paper to Jeronn. She felt humiliated and although Jeronn said nothing had happened she didn't feel any better. However, she had done the exact same thing to him.

"Trace baby I know this is coming at a bad time. And I know that we need to tackle all of this about Retha but what are we going to do about these dudes stalking us?"

"Us?! They are not stalking us Jeronn. They're stalking you. You know ever since you've been in my life everything is just one misunderstanding after the next. Well this is not hard to misunderstand. If she was in the doorway naked, willing to risk all humility just to stick it to me, then I know that you slept with her. Whether you remember it or not. And you know what? I can't say anything. That's your ex-wife. Not me! Her. See how easy it was to get her to marry you? I was with you for years and you wouldn't even consider marrying me. Now your broke down ass wants me and needs me. And I'm supposed to come to your rescue while your ex-wife still has the luxury of taking a dip anytime she feels like it. Oh was she feeling vulnerable again, or was it you this time? I don't need this crap Jeronn. I said I would help you and I would. But after this, don't call me. Don't contact me. I don't ever want to hear from you again. Do you understand me?"

"Trace you don't mean that?"

"I mean that with every cell in my body. You need to get your tired looking self out of my face before I scream."

"Trace what's up? I know you're angry. But you don't have to snap out like this. What if I left for awhile and came back later and we could talk?"

"Fine."

"Okay baby, I'll be back in a couple of hours. I love you Trace and I know we can work this out." When he left, Trace called the front desk and had her room moved. She also booked another room on another floor for Jeronn. She knew he couldn't stay in that hotel on his own finances, so she would give him a place to stay for the night, before she headed back to Miami in the morning. No sense in trying to stay here any longer since she couldn't possibly visit her family with people following Jeronn. She left a message at the front desk for Red to have her new room number. She called her mom and told her something important came up and she was sorry she couldn't make it. She booked 2 first class seats back to Miami, for tomorrow morning. Then she called her financier and had him cut two checks. One to Jeronn's production company and the other to Cash. She had them hand delivered to her home and she would take care of them in the morning. Afterwards she felt sick. She felt like she was on the verge of a breakdown. Why should she be helping him? Why should she feel compassion for someone who hurt her so badly? She knew the media liked to hype things up and make things appear to be what they're not. Although she had to admit, it hurt. Red called Trace on her cellular phone, he was nearing downtown Chicago. She gave him her new room number and said she would explain when he got there.

Chapter Twenty

When Jeronn returned he was a little upset about not being able to get into Trace's room. His card wasn't working. He knocked but there was no answer. He went to the front desk and asked about her checking out. They asked for his name and gave him the card for his room. He assumed she would be in there, but she wasn't. Neither were any of her things. He saw the light on the phone flashing and checked his messages.

Jeronn. Hi it's me. I'm in the hotel, in a different room. I didn't want to take the chance of those guys getting my room number. I got this room for you to stay in tonight so they wouldn't know where to find you either. The room is in a different name so there's nothing for you to worry about. Our flight leaves at 10 a.m. I'll meet you at O'Hare in the morning. There will be a limo waiting to take you there at about 8:45. They'll give you all the flight information. I've also taken the liberty of speaking directly to the CEO at your record company and we've worked out an arrangement. I hope that was ok. Let's see what else? I've gotten a check ready for you to pay off your loan. We'll discuss all that tomorrow. So you wont have anything to worry about anymore. I don't really feel like talking tonight Jeronn, so please don't try and find me. They're not giving out my room

number so please don't try and harass them. If you do, I will switch hotels.
Order anything from room service you need. It's taken care of.

He felt like a chump. He could tell she'd been crying. He had

brought nothing but turmoil in her life since the day he left her and she

was still taking care of everything. He decided to go down to the bar and

have a drink. Since he wasn't going to be able to talk to Trace tonight at

least he could pass out and not have to think about it. He was glad his

debts were going to be settled but that didn't bring much comfort seeing as

how Trace was his only resource.

Graham sat at home the next few days trying to figure out how it

was so easy to make that fast cash and how he was going to spend it. He

couldn't possibly tell Lonnie how he'd gotten the money. He'd almost lost

his life for it. But talking to Red for those two hours seemed profitable.

He was a little upset how everything had started out, but he was going off

pure adrenaline. He had never been a stick up man before. He didn't know

what he was doing. He was a little skeptical about Red just letting him

walk out with all that cash, but he had promised to never return. He was

sure there wasn't two million dollars in that bag though. He had hid the

bag in the back of his closet. Lonnie never looked in his closet. She only cleaned whatever he put in the hamper. He took two hands full of cash and decided to take it to Sonya. When he arrived at her door it took her awhile to answer. He was always worried about coming over here and finding her with somebody. But she was there and she was alone. She was sleeping. When she saw him, her face lit up. She threw her arms him and gave him a big kiss on the cheek.

"Hi Sweetie. Where y'all been?" she gushed.

"Just here and there. Trying to make some money."

"Well can I fix ya somethin' ta eat? Are ya hungry?"

"Actually I'm fine. I'm cool. I came over here to give you a present?"

"Really a present for me? What is it?"

"Close your eyes and open your hands." She did what he'd asked. He placed the bundles of cash in each hand. She opened her eyes. "Oh my God Graham, what is this? What have you done?"

"I just thought I'd bring you a little something to help you get on your feet."

"What have you done? Why did you do this?"

"Well I didn't rob a bank or anything, but I remember how nice you were to me at the restaurant that morning and I just wanted to thank you. I was feeling low that day and you just don't know what you did for me and I just want to say thank you."

"Well sweetie I only did what any normal hospitable person would do. I guess I'll just say thank you. My goodness I can't believe this. Who would've thought I'd wake up to this?" She flopped on the sofa staring at the money. "Well come on darlin'. What do you want to do? We gotta celebrate."

"Well I can't stay. I probably won't be coming back. I just wanted to say thank you for being there and wish you good luck."

"Well Graham, thank you for being here on this day. And good luck to you too." She wrapped her arms around his waste again and watched him down the stairs as he left the building.

Graham was feeling pretty good about himself. He decided to go to the grocery store and pick up dinner for Lonnie and have it ready for her when she got home later. As he was leaving he felt like he was being watched. It felt really weird. Seeing as how Red had given him his card he just knew he wouldn't send anybody after him to hurt him. This had to be something else. When he got home he peeked out the blinds to see if he could see anything. Nothing. He started dinner and gave Red a call on his cell phone. He left a message. *"Uh, Hi. This is Graham Watkins again. I just want to thank you again for uh, letting me uh work for you and um, I look forward to us working together and again I'm sorry for the way I came in there like that. I panicked and I uh, thank you for understanding. Uh you know where to reach me. Uh, hope to be hearing from you soon."*

That was hard to do. He was so nervous. *Why did I say 'uh' so much?* He thought to himself. By the time Lonnie came home, dinner was almost ready. He greeted her with flowers and a card. She was very excited. They had a wonderful evening together and just lay around watching television. Just as they were about to go to bed there was a knock at the door. Lonnie got up to answer it. Two men bombarded past her and rushed in looking for Graham. They dragged him out kicking and screaming. Lonnie was screaming and crying and ran into the bedroom to call the police. She was just about to dial when she felt a heavy object hit her across the back of the head.

Red showed up at the hotel around midnight. Trace peeked through the peephole to be sure it wasn't Jeronn. She had anticipated Red's arrival. She even wore something sexy. She kept telling herself that it was for nothing, but she couldn't help but try and look her best. After confirming her plans with Ross about her dealings with Jeronn's company, she prepared herself for an evening with Red. He called her to tell her he had something to take care of in town before he arrived, but that he would be there. He was actually making sure he was seen out of town and not back in Miami. She told him that Jeronn would be staying in a separate room and she would wait for him. When she opened the door he took her breathe away. He had on leather pants with a leather blazer and a thin white sweater under it. He smelled so good, she could hardly keep her eyes off of him. "Dag girl, it's like that?" he spoke first. "What are you talking about?" she giggled.

"I'm talking about how good you look. Who you doing all that for?"

"Boy, get in here. You are so silly." He took a seat on the sofa and Trace sat next to him. He muted the television. "So how is everything?" She told him about the events of the day and how she ended up in a separate room than before. He asked her if the goons had been around the hotel that she knew of. She didn't know. She wasn't trying to contact Jeronn. She told him they were going to meet at the airport in the morning and they would talk then. "So you want to just hang out here tonight or what?" She smiled. "What did you have in mind?" he asked.

"I don't know. I thought maybe we could go get some good old Harold's chicken while we're here. You know you can't find good chicken like that where we live!" She joked.

"Ok cool. Let me show you some places in Chicago, I know you ain't never been to?"

"Uh-uh. You're not about to take me to some Bi-sexual dance club and try to turn me out are you?"

"Now do I look like I would do something like that?"

"All day long." She teased.

He laughed. "Okay, okay, well do I look like that's something I would do with you?"

"You bet not." She pointed.

"Get ready girl." She changed into a sexy leather dress with a light leather blazer to match what he was wearing. She was really excited to go out with Red. More excited than she expected to be. First the limo took them to Harold's Chicken on the West Side. Then they drove further north to a Reggae club. They listened to some beats and even danced a little. Trace was having so much fun. The nights behind her were a distant memory. Tonight she wasn't thinking about Jeronn or that apartment or anything else. She knew as long as she was with Red she didn't have to worry about thugs beating her up at all. She didn't even worry about the money to help Jeronn out. Tonight she would be free. And tomorrow? Well she'd pick that problem up later. Right now she was having too much fun.

She closed her eyes and let Red put his arms around her. He held her so close. She inhaled his scent and dreamed of him. She closed her eyes and thought about what they had done before. She could tell he was thinking about it too. She could feel it through his pants. They looked in each other's eyes and left the dance floor. Back in the limo they kissed so hard and so fierce, they could have sucked each other's tongues off. They didn't wait to go to the room. They made love right there in the limo. As they were exiting the limousine, Trace held her shoes in her hand and a bottle of wine in the other. Red no longer had on his sweater. Only the leather blazer and the leather pants. He was dripping sex appeal. They laughed all the way to the elevators.

Jeronn was tired of sitting in his room and he didn't want to order room service alone. He called up some friends to hang out with and they came over to his hotel room. He hadn't seen some of these guys since he had left Chicago. They were partying and having a good time. One of his guys brought ladies over to entertain them but Jeronn could only think of Trace. After his friends had left one of the ladies decided to stick around a little longer and keep Jeronn company.

"You look like you just lost your best friend." He just stared at her. Normally in a situation like this it would be on, but he couldn't bring himself to it. Jeronn just stood on the hotel balcony overlooking Lake

Michigan. The wind felt good against his face. It helped him to dream.

"Natalie, maybe you ought to go. I'm really no good company tonight."

"I can see that. But you know what? I don't feel like being alone either."

Natalie wrapped her lace shawl over her shoulders and stood staring at the

lake next to Jeronn. It really was beautiful. The cars down below seemed

a million miles away. They didn't talk. They just held hands and kept

their thoughts.

After a while of this Jeronn said, "It's getting pretty late and I have

to catch a plane in the morning. Can I get you cab?" "Nah. I'm cool. I

can grab a hotel limo. If you're ever in town again Jeronn, call me. This

was nice. It was just what I needed. A little solitude." He smiled. "Well at

least let me see you downstairs."

"That's cool," she smiled. They headed for the elevators. After he

watched her out, he headed for the bar. But before he could get seated on

the stool well, his eyes were bugging out of his head. He couldn't believe

it. Trace was walking in the hotel barefoot and holding Red's hand. They

were laughing and smiling like they didn't have a care in the world. He

marched directly towards the elevators and tried to catch them but the

doors closed too fast. He looked up to see what floor the elevator was

going to but there was no monitor. He was upset. He walked over to the front desk and inquired about what room Trace was in. The clerk looked on the monitor and informed him that he was unable to give that information out.

He was on the verge of losing it. So he opened his wallet. "How much would it take for you to give me that information?" The clerk rolled his eyes and snapped his fingers.

"It won't cost nothing, because I'm not giving out that information. I'm not about to lose my job for every star crazed fool that comes through those doors." Jeronn couldn't hold it in anymore. "Look you gay son of a bitch, I want to know what room Trace Reese is in right now, or you will be in a world of trouble. Do I look star crazed to you? I'm her fiancé, for crying out loud. And I am the CEO of my own record label. Your little 10 dollars an hour job don't mean jack to me."

"Oh no he didn't!" The clerk said to what had to be his imaginary homey. "Did you hear what this fool said to me?" He started rolling his neck and pointing his finger at the same time. "Ain't nobody scerred'a you mista C-E-O. And if Miss Reese was your fiancée you would know what room she was in OK!? And first of all, it didn't look like *you* she strolled in here with five minutes ago, bout to get her freak on OK? So you can just march your happy tail back into the bar or leave her a message. Either way, you betsta get outta my face before I have you removed from this hotel!"

Jeronn's mind played a flash of Red on top of his woman and being seen with his woman and his mind swimming with what he knew was going to go on. On top of all that he had to put up with this guy. "Boy I will come around that counter and whoop yo ass. Do you hear me?"

"Walk away man." The security guard came over. "Just walk away. No need to cause a scene. We don't want that kind of publicity in this hotel sir. Either go in your room or I'm going to have to escort you out." Jeronn looked at the big burly guard and realized he couldn't take him. He was fuming. He mind told him to go to every door and knock until he found Trace. He couldn't take it. He hopped into a cab and headed for a liquor store. Killing Trace was not the furthest thing from his mind.

Chapter Twenty-One

Trace and Red spent a few hours in the Jacuzzi giggling and talking. Trace was having a wonderful time. Red told her how he came to be in the business he was in. He told her way too much information about Mai. But getting a chance to know him proved lucrative. She realized they had a few friends in the same circles and being able to help one another was advantageous. "You do realize that once we leave this room this will be the last time we get together?" she asked.

"Yeah, I thought of that. But I figure with us getting a new business relationship started maybe that wouldn't be true." he replied. She smiled.

"You know what Red? Maybe in another time and another place that would be true. And you know what? You've been so sweet to me, that I know I will always have a soft spot for you. Baby, you've done things to my body that I haven't felt in years. But the truth is, I love Jeronn. And I know you're probably thinking how could that be if I keep calling you right? Well, I do love Jeronn. And I'm going to give it a try. That's all I ever wanted to do. I'm going to help him out of his situation and see where that takes us. But you know what?" she leaned into him. "I had a good time." Red smiled.

"Yeah, me too. Well you know I'm not going to be getting my heart involved and all that, but the truth is you're a wonderful woman. And you probably would be just the woman to settle Dirty Red down, but I guess I'm not that lucky."

Trace got out of the Jacuzzi and lay on the bed. Red rubbed lotion all over her body. By the time he got to her toes they were making love again. She tried to block Jeronn from her thoughts, but she was feeling too sober. Afterwards, they lie in each other's arms and fell asleep. Neither one knowing that death could befall them the next day.

Jeronn parked his rental car across the street from the hotel. He waited in the car until morning to see Trace and Red leave the hotel. He was going to kill one or the both of them. He didn't know which one. He had been drinking and getting high and crying all night. He didn't know what he was doing. All he knew is that he hurt and he wanted the hurt to go away. If Trace wasn't going to be completely his then she wasn't going to be anybody's. The sun was burning his eyes and the tears had stopped falling. Every time he had a fresh image of last night and thought about what Trace and Red were doing it cut him more. He tried to rationalize that maybe Trace and Red met up coincidentally, but then why were they holding hands. He tried to think that maybe they had separate rooms, but the desk clerk wouldn't give him any information after the way he acted. He looked at the clock on the dash. It showed that he had one and half-hours before the plane was scheduled to take off. He was steeling himself to confront Trace. He cocked the gun on his lap. He watched Red leaving the hotel. Walking like he hadn't a care in the world. He didn't see Trace. He didn't care. He got out of the car with the gun to his side and walked briskly across the street. He pointed the gun.

"Stay right there playa." Red stared Jeronn in the eyes. "Jay, man, don't do something you're going to regret."

"What nigga? You lay up in a hotel with my woman all night and you telling me about regrets! I think you're the one with regrets fool. I'm about to prove that to you right now."

"Jay. Put the gun down man. You don't know what you're doing." Red had his hands faced out toward Jeronn. "Jeronn listen to me."

"No you listen. You're always a calm talking dude ain't you? Nothing gets Dirty Red upset does it?"

"Jeronn! Listen to me. You're standing right outside my limo. Now you know I don't go anywhere alone. Right inside that limo is a gun pointed right at your guts man. I know the windows are tinted but trust me. You don't want these kinds of problems. So why don't you put the gun down and let's handle this like men." Jeronn looked at his image in the window.

He couldn't see anything inside, but he knew Red wouldn't bluff like that. He started rocking back and forth. He didn't want to die. He wanted Red to die. He continued to hold the gun on Red, but he was feeling antsy. "Why did you do it man?" He moaned.

"Jeronn, you're calling attention to us. We don't want to do this man. Let's talk this out. Trace will be out here in a minute and you already know she doesn't want this kind of attention. Don't do it man."

"Shut the hell up. Don't tell me what my woman wants. You don't know!" He was crying. "You don't know."

"Well I know." Trace appeared out of nowhere. Jeronn was startled. He pointed the gun at Trace.

"Trace, how could you do this to me? I thought you loved me?"

"Jeronn, baby, don't do this. Put that gun down. Look at you honey. What is this all about?"

"You spent the night with this nigga. I know you did."

"Jeronn, we stayed in the same room together yes, but it was only for protection."

"What? You expect me to believe that? This the second time you and him got together." He yelled.

"Jeronn listen to me. People are watching me. Now I'm about to get in this cab and go to the airport. You can put that gun down and go with me, or you can shoot me in the damned back because I'm not about to stand here and give all these people something to talk about. Good bye Jeronn."

"Trace don't move," he pleaded. Trace marched towards a cab. She turned around and looked at him once.

"Drive." she told the driver. And she was gone. While his back was to Red, Red had hopped in his own limo and told the driver to pull off. Red was gone without a word. Jeronn was left standing in the middle of the street holding a gun and looking like a fool.

A crowd had gathered around him and he could hear police sirens. He hopped in his rental car and headed for the airport. He figured if the police followed him he could ditch them on the interstate. When he got to the airport, he left the car at a paid parking ramp. He didn't return it to the rental company. He went into the men's room and composed himself. He wanted to look as well as he could when he got on the plane with Trace. When he got to the ticket counter Trace was nowhere to be seen. He picked up his first class ticket and waited on the plane. Trace never arrived. He flew back to Miami.

Trace had the cabdriver take her to Midway airport rather than O'Hare. She had every intention of taking the charter back with Red. She had tried to call Jeronn's room several times that morning, but there was never an answer. She was going to tell him she would meet him back in Miami. Seeing him in front of the hotel wielding a gun put a horrible fright in her. She felt sick to her stomach. Moments after her cab arrived at Midway airport, Red's limo pulled up. As always, he was one step ahead of her. She and Red boarded the plane in silence. There was nothing to say. An exciting adventure had turned into a painful nightmare. She leaned back with her eyes closed. Thinking about Jeronn and how far over the edge he had gone. She didn't know what to make of it. She and Red had talked about Jeronn and their future all night. She had nothing to say to him right now. Red had learned a lot of shameful things about her in a very short time. Out of all he had learned, he never judged her. She appreciated that. The flight to Miami was only a couple of hours. She nodded off.

Trace walked down the long aisle. This was the day she had been waiting for. She and Jeronn were getting married. She wore a long, white flowing gown. All her family and friends were there. People she had known since she was a child smiled and waited to see her marry Jeronn. The further she got down the aisle, the further away Jeronn seemed to be. All of a sudden, she didn't feel bad. She felt joy. She felt excited inside. She made her way into the choir stand. She was no longer wearing a wedding dress, but a choir robe. It was glowing. She was the lead singer in the choir and she was singing. There were no record execs. No adoring fans. Only friends and family who loved her. She looked to the back of the church and Jeronn was there. He was holding her daughter's hand. They were smiling at her and worshipping the Lord. The sun was shining on her face and she began to sing. She felt free. The Lord had lifted her burdens and she was free. Just as she was about to shout she heard the preacher speak. "Buckle your seatbelts and prepare for landing...."

Trace stirred awake. She had had a wonderful dream. She smiled at Red. "Everything okay? You were smiling in your sleep."

"Everything's fine now. I'm back home and I'll be seeing my daughter and my grandbaby soon and everything is just fine." He smiled at her. "Trace I'm sure everything will be fine with you and Jeronn. Just give it time. I don't know what went on back there at the hotel, but rest assured for your sake, I won't be doing anything to retaliate against him. I was with his woman all night. He was justifiably angry." He laughed.

"I know. I'm going to give it some time. I'll be in touch if I need you okay?"

"Sure." he replied.

"Anthony Jones. My goodness. Thank you for everything. You have been absolutely wonderful. Above all, you've been a gentleman and I thank you. Thank you for helping me put my old life behind me and face the new one." He held her hand.

"Thank you Trace. For snapping me out of my own world and giving me a taste of the real world. Of course, the real world is too real for me so like you said, I probably won't see you again. Maybe in professional circles, but not on a personal level. I guess if I ever want to settle down, you'd be the type of woman I would want." He held her.

"Well thank you. That was quite a compliment. And you know what else? I'm going to pray for you. I'm going to pray that you find whatever you're looking for. This is not the life for you. And that's all I'm going to say."

He escorted her off the plane and into a waiting limousine. That would be the last time Trace talked to Red. She waved out of the window as the limo pulled off. He blew her a kiss with the peace sign. He was going to miss her.

Chapter Twenty-Two

Graham and Lonnie woke up in unfamiliar surroundings. They looked around the warehouse in the darkness. They were frightened.

"Graham. What is going on here? I'm scared." Graham licked his lips. "Baby don't be scared." He got up from the floor. He tried to comfort her. They held hands walking towards the exit.

"Graham, what do you think is happening?"

"I don't know." He held her hand tightly. There was nothing outside. There was an envelope taped to the door with his name on it.

You're a very lucky young man. The lady had sympathy on you and I promised her I wouldn't hurt you. If you know what's good for you and your lady you will stay where you are and not return to Miami. Your loot is in the duffel bag behind you. If I run across you again son, you might not be so lucky. D.R.

"Graham, who in the hell is D. R. and what is he talking about? What lady had sympathy on you? What loot? And where in the hell are we?"

Graham couldn't answer her last question. "I don't know where we are, but we better get out of here." he responded.

"What? Graham, what is going on here? I don't see a duffel bag," she cried.

"It's right here. I found it. Baby are you alright?"

"My damn head hurts and I'm getting pissed because I know you know what's going on here and you're pissing me off even more!" she was yelling.

"I'll explain everything when we get out of here. We have to find out where we are?" Graham grabbed Lonnie's hand and led her into the sunlight. As they approached the curb a large man in a suit walked up to him.

"Are you Graham Watkins?"

"Who wants to know?" he quipped.

"Get in the car."

"We will not!" Lonnie screamed.

"Lonnie just get in the car." Graham pushed.

"Can I get an explanation for all this?" He asked.

"Yeah. You agreed to work for Mr. Red right?"

"Mr. Who?" Lonnie argued.

"Lonnie wait a minute okay? Let me ask the questions."

"Well you need to hurry the hell up and tell me what's going on," she argued.

"I agreed to work for Red, but that doesn't explain why me and my wife were knocked out and brought here. And where are we?"

"You're in L.A."

"L.A.!?" They both yelled. "How in the hell we get all the way across the map?"

"You agreed to work for Red in exchange for your life. Would you like to retract your offer?" the thug smiled. Lonnie looked at Graham in disbelief. "Graham what is he talking about?" She was scared. He found out his name was Reggie and that he would work directly for him. He didn't notice Lonnie had unzipped his duffel bag.

"Graham where in the world did all this money come from?" He snatched the money and the bag away from her. The driver dropped them off in front of a small cottage house. "Where are we?" Graham asked.

"Home. Get out." Reggie ordered.

"What does he mean home?" Lonnie started crying. "I want to talk to Red." Graham demanded. Red will be in touch with you when he's ready to be in touch with you. Now take your wife and your money into your new home and start living. I'll be in touch with you regarding your new job." He closed the door to the backseat and hopped in the front seat. Lonnie stood in front of the house in disbelief. She couldn't stop crying. Graham stood next to the driver's door and asked Reggie in disbelief.

"What are we doing here? Why are we being made to live here?"

"You don't threaten Red's life and expect to get off. The only reason you're alive is because he promised he would let you live and he's a man of his word. If you return to Miami for any reason at all, without letting Red know you're coming, that's it. You're life is over. Literally. What you're doing is nothing compared to what you could be doing. So enjoy your life in L.A. It's not all that bad. I'll be in touch." He drove away. Graham stood in the doorway of the new house. He was in shock. He never knew that anything like this would come of his mistake. He had planned to leave town anyway, but to force Lonnie to go and make her live a life that she hadn't chosen was the last thing he wanted to do. She was stuck here with him and there wasn't anything he could do about it.

Lonnie cried for weeks. They tried to piece a life together from scratch, but it was hard. They used a lot of the money to buy things they needed. Red hadn't supplied them with anything. He finally got a call from Red after a few weeks. "Enjoying your new digs?" He could tell Red was smiling through the phone. "Red. Sir. Why am I here?" For the first time in years Graham wanted to cry.

"Motherfucker don't ask me no stupid questions. You're lucky you have a roof over your head. If you weren't married I'd have you living in a cardboard box. That money would be doing nothing for you. But since you surprised me with a wife I decided to do you the honor of bringing her with you and letting you see how it feels to see a woman in pain. You hurt my friend, which means you hurt me. You will work for me until I see fit to let you loose. In the meantime, live right nigga. Remember, you could be dead." He hung up.

Graham finally regretted doing what he did. It finally hit him, all the time and effort he put into hurting that woman and now Red hurt his wife and there was nothing he could do about it. It was either do what he said, or lose his life. Not only his, but Lonnie's. After Graham had told Lonnie what he had done, she wasn't the same. She didn't look at him the same. She couldn't imagine someone she loved so much could be so in love with money that he would threaten someone's life personally and physically. She knew she would always love Graham, but she would never love him like she used to.

The next couple of weeks went by in a blur for Trace. She had done her share of crying. Singing always put her in a good mood. Singing and crying washed her blues away. One Sunday after she had done all the crying she could do, she went to church. Chanelle offered to go with her but Trace needed to be alone. She wanted to be alone with the Lord. She wanted to sit in the back of the church unnoticed and pour out her heart to the Father. She loved the Lord. She felt grateful for all he had done for her in her life all these years. When she arrived there it felt just like home. She sat in the back of the church and listened to the choir sing. They were singing an old song, '*I Love to Praise Him.*' She held in the tears until she couldn't hold them any longer. She wept. She cried for all the pain she had locked inside. She cried for all the love that she had lost. She cried for all the love she had thrown away. For all the time she had thrown away. She cried for all the pain she put on others. She cried for Jeronn's pain. She cried for his addictions. She cried for her soul. She praised God for protecting her all these years while she had been doing wrong. She praised God for giving her grace in her world of sin. She thanked Him for mercy. She wrenched her hands and lifted her arms because her body could no longer hold on. The people around her praised the Lord with her. Trace stood on her feet and opened her eyes to the sky. She lifted her hands and cried 'thank you' repeatedly. She couldn't stop. The tears fell from the corners of her eyes. Her joyful heart filled with love. Peace consumed her body. She could let go now. She could let go of all the pain. She could let go of humiliation. She could let go of despair. She could let go of hopelessness. She could let go of hate. She let it all go and gave it to the Lord. She could feel His presence. She cherished it. She never wanted the feeling to end. She was home.

Jeronn submerged himself in his work. After that gun show he figured he'd never see Trace again. What right did he have to make demands on her or to put her through his hell? He had gotten himself in every situation that he was in and he was determined to get himself out. He didn't move all the way out here to fail. That was never an option. Being in the studio all the time began to pay off for him. He was making money and getting his life together. Trace had taken care of all his business just like she said she would. And she did it all without having any contact with him. His name was becoming hot again. After not seeing Trace for a while he never thought he'd ever feel this happy again, but it was happening. It was hard at first, but when days turned into weeks he decided he would wait until she was ready to be a part of his life. In the meantime, he cleaned house. Retha was constantly hounding him about hooking up for sex. She laughed hysterically on his answering machine when she found out that he and Trace had split up. She was tickled by it. He told her they would never ever get together again and she was the last person in the world he'd ever want to have sex with as long as he lived. She had showed up at his door once wearing nothing but a trench coat. He slammed the door in her face. She was so intrigued by him making a name for himself again that she was wearing her greed on her sleeve. She sent him a letter and he wrote on the envelope 'return to hoochie, address unknown'. He felt sorry for leaving Trace for a relationship with Retha. After a little more time had gone by, he had tried to call Trace on several occasions but she was always busy, not home or simply didn't want to talk. He went to her private apartment once but noticed there were no blinds or anything in the window and realized she really had cleaned the place out. One morning he decided to go for a jog and instead drove his car to her neighborhood to watch her leaving for church. She was gorgeous. She was wearing her beautiful black hair in a bun. She was breathtaking. He waited until she was out of sight and drove back home. He thought of calling Red on occasion to talk and apologize or just to hang out, but decided against it. He knew he owed him an apology but he also knew Red wouldn't think much of it. He would probably hurt somebody else, for what he did, but not Jeronn. He also knew that if he had hung out with Red he knew he would for sure get high. He had talked to Chanelle a few times and she told him that things were pretty normal. Her mom was home a lot more and scheduling fewer engagements for the year. She was spending more time with the baby while Chanelle went to school. He was happy for her. But he missed her dearly.

Trace missed Jeronn as well. She desperately wanted them to work things out but traces of the humiliation and pain still lingered in her mind. She worked hard to forgive him every time sporadic visions of Jeronn and Retha popped in her head. And she prayed he could forgive her. This was the woman he had come to Florida with. Trace had dreams about Retha and Jeronn making love right in front of her. She knew she wasn't ready to deal with him. She started singing in church again and it was chicken soup for her soul. She spent more time with her friends and less time hurting over the ways of the past. She ran into Red at a party or two, but she couldn't bring herself to say hello. She avoided him at all costs. Red made her body weak and she couldn't afford to be a part of that life anymore. Red really was a special friend. He kept her secret and he somehow took care of the man who was going to kill her about it. She didn't know how, and she didn't want to know. She would owe him her life for that. Trace's birthday was coming up though and she knew she should invite him to the party. Ross was helping her plan it. They had developed a better relationship after she set him straight.

Red sent her a card during her sabbatical from Jeronn. She appreciated the gesture. She laughed when she read it because she couldn't imagine Red standing in Hallmark picking out a card for her. But he assured her in the card that he did. She knew she would have to invite Red. It was a 'whose who' sort of affair. Everyone on the A list in the music business was going to be there. She wanted Jeronn to be there to share her day. She personally wrote him an invitation and prayed for him to be there. Ross had everything flown in from the food to the flowers, to the clothes she would wear. Trace couldn't wait. She missed Jeronn and she wanted to look good. She got up early to go for a jog. Afterwards, she went for a massage and to get her hair done. Ross went over the list of people to arrive, so there were no party crashers. Red hadn't confirmed, but she knew he would be there. She put his name on the list. The servers and the valet were in place. Everything was set.

One hour before party time, Trace was sitting in the kitchen looking things over as the caterers buzzed about. The lawn was impeccable. Lights along the walkway, led the way to a huge tent in the back of the house. Guests were to arrive at the front and be escorted into the back. Nothing was left undone. Ross arrived early to make sure everything was in order and to introduce Trace to the woman in his life. He was very proud of her. He had been dating her for a few weeks and had grown quite fond of her. She was a realtor and she had sold him his current home. She was beautiful. She was especially delighted to meet Trace. Chanelle told her mom, it was really time to get ready. Her make up was done and everything was ready except her. Trace stepped into her bedroom and admired her dress on the bed. It was similar to the black dress she wore the night she met Jeronn. Ross had had it flown in from Milan and she couldn't wait to put it on. The dress was stunning. It was a far cry from the twenty-dollar hoochie mama dress she wore twenty years ago at the club. The night she met Jeronn. She smiled at the memory. She descended the stairs and went to the back. Many guests had arrived already. Her gift table was overflowing. She loved gifts. She greeted many in her search for Jeronn. He had yet to arrive. After an hour, she wondered if he would even show up. Chanelle toasted her guests and they sang happy birthday to her mother. They wheeled out a six-tier birthday cake with what looked like a hundred candles. She laughed as she and Chanelle tried to blow them out. She thought she saw Jeronn in the crowd, but she couldn't find him. She wasn't going to feel bad. Not tonight. It was her birthday. As she was headed for the ladies room, Red stopped her in the hall. He was on his cellular phone and he hung up on whomever he was talking to.

"Well, well, women certainly do get better with age." She smiled. "Hi Red." she smiled.

"My, my my you look so good girl." He replied.

"Eat your heart out?"

"What? Eat what out?"

"Ooh Red. Don't go there. I'm so glad you could make it." She was grinning from ear to ear.

"Well I'm so glad to be invited to such a personal and special event." Charming as usual. "I see you haven't changed." She was referring to his entourage of women.

"Hey what can I say? You know I like to get dirty-dirty."

"And with that I think I'll greet some more guests." She briefly held his hands and walked away. Some things may never change, she thought. After another hour or so her friends asked her to sing a song for them. They coaxed her into it even though it was her own birthday party. Chanelle stood right in front. She loved to hear her mom sing. As her song was ending, she felt a sense of de'javu. Jeronn seemed to be floating through the crowd coming her way. She closed her eyes and when she opened them again, he was gone. As her friends and well-wishers hugged her and toasted her happy birthday, she felt him behind her. "Was that song for me?" She smiled and faced him. "Baby, everything about me is for you?"

"Is that right? Well may I have this dance please?"

"I don't see why not?"

"So what are you doing after the party?"

She laughed. "Going home with my friend?" His voice was still smooth like butter.

"Well why don't you let me take your friend home and take you to breakfast?"

"I don't know. I've been down this road before and it was too bumpy."

"Well this time I want to make it easier Trace. I want a chance to make all your dreams come true. And this time, I promise, you wont get any drama from me."

"Jeronn Montarius Clark? What are you talking about?"

"I'm talking about this." He pulled a ring from his pocket.

"I'm talking about you becoming Trace Clarke? Baby, will you do me the honors of making the journey of my weary soul come to an end by becoming my wife?" Tears filled her eyes. Chanelle and Maja watched the whole scene in the distance. They cried too. Ross smiled. Red tipped his glass. Trace said yes. "Yes, yes. Oh baby, yes."

The End